IN OVER HER HEAD

CORPORATE CHAOS SERIES BOOK 1

LEIGHANN DOBBS
LISA FENWICK

Marly West rushed down the hallway at Draconia Fashions, rubbing vigorously at the stained lapel of her crisp white blouse with a wet napkin. The egg sandwich she had scarfed down at breakfast roiled in her stomach as she picked up the pace, practically breaking into a jog.

Please don't let me be late.

She rounded the corner, shoving the wet napkin into her notebook, which she then clutched against her chest.

The conference room loomed at the end of the hallway. Through the floor-to-ceiling windows, she could see the gigantic table surrounded by black leather chairs —all filled with various company executives. Sunlight flooded in from the windows against the wall, which revealed a breathtaking view of New York City from their vantage point of twenty stories up. But Marly wasn't interested in the view. Her eyes flew to the clock at the head of the table. Five of eight. A sigh of relief pushed past her lips. She wasn't late.

She quietly swung the glass door open and slid into the nearest seat, the supple leather creaking slightly as she settled back into the chair, almost as if to make herself invisible—which, in fact, was exactly her intention. Best to fly under the radar, she told herself. That way no one would suspect her real motives.

Marly slid her notebook onto the polished mahogany table and opened it, studying the pages instead of looking around at the others—perfectly groomed men in Armani suits, stick-thin women in Chanel. By contrast, her own outfit didn't stack up. She'd graduated from college years ago, but payments on her expensive school loans for the dual master's degree in fashion design and marketing didn't leave room for buying expensive clothes. Not that she was complaining. That dual degree was what had landed her this job.

She wondered what the others at the table would think if they knew she'd picked up her outfit from the local thrift store. The navy suit was an expensive label and a flattering cut, if a little outdated. But she hadn't had much to choose from, and it was hard to find a suit that fit her curvy figure—a problem the stick-slim women around the table probably never had experienced. She looked down at herself, noticing how her big boobs strained against the fabric and threatened to pop the buttons open. A flash of self-consciousness ran through her, and she tugged the edges of the jacket together to cover more of her ample chest.

The door in the back of the room opened, and all heads turned in anticipation of the arrival of the CEO, Jasper Kenney. Marly tucked the stained lapel inside her jacket. She'd heard that Kenney was a stickler about perfection, the type that liked everything to be in "its place." One who wouldn't think twice about firing someone on the spot. She didn't want the stained lapel to draw his attention or his disapproval. She needed this job desperately and didn't want to risk anything that might jeopardize it.

It wasn't Kenney who came through the door, though. It was his assistant, Veronica St. James. Her makeup was done to perfection, her shiny blond hair pulled back in a tight chignon. Not a hair out of place, Marly noticed as she pushed a long, dark unruly curl out of her own face.

She watched Veronica set down a pad of paper, several pens, and a coffee cup, taking care to place them precisely in some predesigned spot on the table as if she were putting out a place setting at Buckingham Palace.

As she watched Veronica, Marly's thoughts drifted to the CEO. She'd only been employed by Draconia Fashions for a little over a month and had never actually seen Jasper Kenney. Even though he was an icon in the fashion industry and had been pictured in many fashion magazines and tabloids, Marly had never paid attention. Celebrities weren't her thing.

She'd heard the rumors, though. Jasper Kenney was a shark in the boardroom who kept tight control on his company, and a man who liked beautiful women and went through them as quickly as most people went through a roll of paper towels. He had a quick temper and nitpicky personality, but most people seemed to forgive those traits in the CEO, who was rumored to be a visionary in the fashion industry.

The door opened, and a drop-dead gorgeous man came through. Was that Jasper Kenney? He was much younger than she'd expected—maybe in his early thirties. Tall, probably over six feet, and broad-shouldered, with curly brown hair a little too long for a CEO. But what really got to her were his eyes—a light sky blue and as cold as the shark he was rumored to be.

Marly shrank back in her seat as Kenney sat down at the head of the table. He nodded to Veronica, who filled his coffee cup with the dark brew. Swirls of steam rose from the cup toward the ceiling, and the heavy, bitter smell of coffee drifted down toward Marly.

"Morning, everyone." His deep voice sent a blast of cold dread through Marly. She bit her bottom lip and focused on the meeting agenda sheet that Veronica was passing out. "I expect we can get right to item one."

As the other executives briefed him on the agenda items, Kenney answered in short, clipped tones. He addressed each matter with cold, calculated precision and didn't waste one word. Marly was glad she wouldn't have to speak about any of the items. Her task was just to attend and take notes for her department—a job she had planned to do in utter silence... until she dropped her pen.

It clattered onto the table, stopping all conversation.

Crap, crap, crap!

"Sorry." Marly grimaced as she reached across to retrieve the pen. She glanced up at the head of the table, and her eyes locked with Jasper Kenney's. He held her gaze for a moment longer than normal, and her heart jerked in her chest.

The force of his gaze froze her in mid-reach for the pen, and the stained lapel chose that moment to pop out of her jacket. Kenney's eyes flicked to the lapel. His forehead creased in a small frown before his eyes returned to hers for one last brief second.

Marly grabbed her pen and sank back in her chair, her stomach flipping.

She couldn't be sure, but she thought she saw *something* in Jasper's eyes. It was just a flicker, but it almost looked like interest. No, that couldn't be it—men didn't show interest in *her*. Even though she'd lost fifty pounds this year, she was still too curvy to attract attention from most of them. In her experience, men only wanted skinny girls with fake boobs and spray-on tans like the millions of women who probably threw themselves after rich, successful, gorgeous Jasper Kenney every day.

More than likely, it was disgust. He'd seen the stain on her shirt and was probably right now figuring out whom he would have to contact to have her fired. But she couldn't shake the feeling that his look meant more than that—it was almost as if he had looked right into her soul. Almost as if he could see the *real* reason she was working there.

She focused on her notes, keeping her head down and trying to avoid any more eye contact. Her heart was beating so fast, she was positive everyone could hear it. Her mouth was so dry she could barely swallow, but she was afraid to reach for the water pitcher that was set out for fear one of her klutzy maneuvers would cause her to spill it all over the place. Thankfully, the meeting was almost over. Only the sales department was left to review the monthly numbers.

"This is a disappointment," Jasper said as the vice president of sales explained that the numbers had come in slightly below expectations. "What went wrong? The top fashion magazines all reviewed this line favorably, and we had several nods from A-list celebrities." It was clear by his tone that he was not happy, and glancing around the room, Marly noticed that most of the sales people were looking down at their notes to avoid eye contact.

"Well, we aren't exactly sure what happened, sir. The reviews were all great, and yes, we were featured in several magazines with A-listers wearing the new line out and about." Beads of sweat had formed on Bill Henderson, the VP of sales', upper lip.

Jasper shot Bill a dark look, and Marly could see the older man wither under it. Like most powerful men, it seemed that Jasper Kenney didn't need to use words to get across his message of disapproval.

Looking over the numbers, Marly wasn't surprised that sales were off. They'd created the line for the late-twenty-something crowd, but the prices were too steep. Marly had a decent job there and she, herself, couldn't afford it.

Paying seven hundred dollars for a pair of dress pants or a thousand dollars for a skirt was not what the average person just starting their career would pay. The Hollywood crowd, yes, but this line had been created for the average young woman who was just starting out. Marly knew that if they could lower the price by twenty percent, they would exceed sales. That price range still kept Draconian in the "high scale" clothing level they wanted to be in, but was easier to swallow for the consumer.

"Well, maybe the styles are wrong for that age group," Jasper said, looking around the room as he tossed the binder that contained the sales figures onto the conference room table.

"It isn't the styles. It's the price," Marly butted in— shocked to hear the words come out of her mouth. What was she thinking? Had she really said that out loud?

Every head in the room turned to look at her. Her cheeks burned, and her heart skipped in her chest.

Jasper Kenney narrowed his ice-blue eyes at her. "The price? Miss—"

A lump of sand lodged in Marly's throat.

"West. Marly West," she croaked, waiting for him to tell her to leave and pick up her last paycheck on the way out.

"Well, Miss Marly West, why don't you tell us why

you think it's the prices." Jasper's eyes drilled into hers. He took a sip of coffee and settled back into his over-sized leather chair. Was that a smirk on his face? She couldn't be sure.

Marly took a deep breath. She wished she had poured herself that glass of water. Her hands were shaking, and her heart leaped into her throat. She felt light-headed. She swallowed hard past the lump. Had she really inter-rupted the great Jasper Kenney?

She took a deep breath and started, "The styles all received nothing but positive feedback—we know that. This is the first time that Draconia has had a line specifi-cally geared toward the young career woman." She paused and poured that glass of water, her confidence rising. "The prices are too high for that age range, aside from the A-listers you've already mentioned, and the few and far between who are already in the mid-six-figure income at that age. If you lower the prices, sales will increase as more young women can afford the clothing, but you'll still be able to maintain the high-scale level for the clothing line. In addition, these young women will then move onto our classic line as they grow older and advance in their careers."

"That's quite interesting, Miss...what was your name again?" Jasper's lips quirked in a devilish grin, and Marly could only assume he was having fun at her expense. She wanted to run from the room. She was positive everyone was wondering how she could possibly know anything about the type of fashion the company sold—their clothes were made for the perfectly put-together size-two stick figure, not a voluptuous girl like her with a stain on her lapel.

She started to think about what companies she could send her resume to, as she was sure the next words she would hear would be, "You're fired."

"Marly West," Marly said softly. She willed away the tears that pricked the backs of her eyes. She didn't want the whole office to think she was incapable of talking to this man, and truth be told, she had way more important things to cry over than a botched sales meeting.

"Well, Marly West, you might be on to something. Our line has been successful because we've always catered to the more established crowd. I don't know how much research sales and marketing did on this new line. Given the budgets I approved, I expected much more from them. Write up your summary and what your ideas are on the price reductions as well as how you think we should roll them out to the masses without causing a major clusterfuck in the industry."

He pushed himself up from the table and strode out of the room.

Marly sat there stunned while the sales and marketing people shot dirty looks at her. No one said a word to her. She thought she heard someone say something about telling the new girl to mind her own business, but she wasn't sure.

She gathered her things and headed back to her desk, hating herself for opening her mouth in the first place. She was supposed to be sitting on the sidelines, quietly biding her time until she could act on the *real* reason for taking the job.

But her big mouth had gotten her into trouble, and instead of being invisible, she was now a target—smack-dab in the middle of Jasper Kenney's radar.

2

As Marly walked quietly through the maze of cubicles back toward her desk, her phone dinged. Looking down, she tensed. It was a text from Tanner Durcotte—the last person she wanted to be contacting her at work. The text was a series of question marks.

Not now, Tanner!

She replied as quickly as her fingers would swipe. She just wanted to get back to the safety of her cube before she said or did anything else stupid.

As she sat down, her phone went off again—more from Tanner. He was relentless. He wouldn't stop bothering her until she gave him an update. She was starting to text him back when the hairs on the back of her neck stood up. Spinning around in her chair, she saw Veronica St. James, Jasper's executive assistant, standing behind her.

Marly's heart stuttered. She slid her phone into her

pocket. How long had Veronica been standing there? Had she seen what Marly had been texting to Tanner?

"Oh … hi," Marly mumbled, straightening her skirt and making sure the phone was hidden safely in her pocket as she stood up.

"Mr. Kenney would like to ensure you understand that the information he requested from you be finished and on his desk by eight p.m. tonight," Veronica said dryly. She ran her fingers over Marly's jacket that was hanging up behind her. Marly had hung the jacket up so hastily that it was backwards, with the label and, more embarrassingly, the size showing. The double-digit number glared at her, and she knew Veronica, who was probably a size nothing, saw it. "Nice coat. I didn't realize they made them that big," Veronica said, almost giggling.

Flashbacks of high school ran through Marly's head, and the pain of hurt feelings came flooding back. She'd been quite heavy back then and was often tormented by the other girls for being overweight. Now, she was fifty pounds lighter, and she was still being made fun of. When would it stop? She forced herself to stop thinking about the rude comments and focus on work. She had so much at stake, she needed to stay on track.

"To be able to do what Mr. Kenney asked, I need access to some of the other departments' databases," Marly said with confidence. "Oh, and I also need the last twelve months' financials and sales reports." She held eye contact with Veronica, whose dark, beady eyes registered a hint of surprise. Marly got the distinct impression that Veronica thought she was incompetent. The executive assistant was definitely giving off I-don't-like-you vibes, and Marly had no idea why.

"Well, then, I will make sure that you are given access immediately. Someone from IT will be contacting you with passwords," Veronica said.

Maroon 5 blared from Marly's pocket. *Damn it, Tanner!*

"I'll let you get back to your *phone*," Veronica said sarcastically, and with that, she spun around and sauntered out of the cubicle maze on her six-inch Louboutin heels.

Marly stuck her tongue out behind Veronica's back before she fished her phone out of her pocket and sank back into her chair.

I am making progress. Will advise more later. No time to discuss right now.

She'd hoped that would hold Tanner off for a little bit but also knew it wouldn't be for long. Tanner Durcotte was not a patient man. He hadn't gotten to where he was in life by being patient—or by being nice, for that matter.

She had to come up with a way to placate Tanner and buy herself some time until she could figure out how to get access to the information she really needed.

———

MARLY'S STOMACH grumbled at four thirty, and she realized she hadn't eaten since the egg sandwich at breakfast. She'd been so wrapped up in the reports that the whole day had almost passed. That hardly ever happened.

Maybe working here would be good for her weight loss goals. She grabbed her wallet and headed toward the elevator, hoping to make it to the cafeteria before they closed.

The elevator door whooshed open to reveal Jasper Kenney.

Marly froze. Should she get in with him? Nervous energy rushed through her as she stared at him. He gave off an air of power that was distracting... and seductive. Especially in his crisp white shirt, the sleeves rolled up to the elbow, revealing muscular forearms. She noticed his large, strong hands. Her stomach did a slow, burning roll.

He cocked his eyebrow and asked "Going down?" Then stuck his hand out to stop the door from shutting.

Marly realized she'd been just standing there like an office bimbo.

"Oh, yes, sorry!" She stepped into the elevator, wanting to just crawl into a hole and disappear.

When she leaned over to press the G button on the panel, Jasper did as well. Their fingers collided, and Marly jerked hers away as if she'd been stung. Her heart raced, and she felt dizzy, although she blamed it on the lack of food all day.

Pull it together, she told herself and took a deep breath. She was alone in the elevator with the big boss. Now was as good a time as any to talk to him about the reports.

"I'm almost finished with the reports for you, Mr. Kenney. I'm just grabbing a quick bite and then planned on bringing them up to you, if that's okay?" Marly asked as the elevator rapidly approached the ground floor.

"That'll be fine, Miss West. I'm very eager to see what you've done." The elevator doors opened up, and he stretched his arm out for her to exit first.

Marly stepped out of the elevator, wondering why the fact that he had remembered her name made her feel both giddy and terrified. If she'd only kept her big mouth shut, she could have just flown under the radar. Now he knew her name, she was doing special work for him, and if the things she'd heard about him were true, one minor screwup could get her fired.

She turned around to ask him if she should contact Veronica when she was ready to bring the reports to him, as she didn't have access to his floor, and as she did, she caught him eyeing her behind.

She quickly spun her head back around. *Oh my God.* Was he checking her out?

She hurried away in a haze of self-consciousness, wondering if he was still looking. And why would he?

Could he be interested in her? No, that was silly. He was a hot, rich CEO and her boss's boss's boss.

Then it dawned on her—she must have sat on something. How humiliating. She probably had a big stain on her butt and he was too disgusted to tell her. This was so embarrassing. She ran into the bathroom and twisted herself around to look in the mirror, expecting to see a big stain on her butt. There was nothing there.

She looked at herself in the mirror, taking in her dark-brown hair, which was too unruly to be cut into one of the latest fashionable styles all the other girls at Draconia seemed to be wearing, her plain, boring brown eyes, and her oversized body, which practically burst out of her outfit.

Jasper Kenney was one of the most eligible bachelors in the state. Why would he be checking someone like her out?

He wouldn't. The only guys that had shown an interest in her before had turned out to be unfaithful losers. Angry thoughts of her last boyfriend, Derek, speared her heart. She'd trusted him, and he'd thrown that all away. Better off to be alone. She splashed cold water on her face and headed to the cafeteria, convincing herself that the lack of food was affecting her common sense and causing her to imagine things that just weren't there.

JASPER TRIED to stop the thoughts racing through his head as he watched the elevator doors slide shut. He was used to being around beautiful women. In fact, he'd dated some of the most beautiful women on the planet, but Marly West intrigued him.

He wasn't sure why. She wasn't perfectly put together like the models he favored. Her hair was unruly, her outfit outdated, and she had a bit more padding. Maybe that was what he liked about her—those bony models who were always spending hours in front of the mirror could get tedious.

And then there were her insights into the clothing line that she'd shared in the meeting. She'd shown intelligence and initiative. He liked that. But most of all she'd shown that she had the balls to speak up to him and suggest that they might have made a mistake. None of the other ass-kissing sales people ever did that. It got boring after a while when everyone yessed you to death.

It would be nice to have a professional relationship with someone that he could trust to be honest when he bounced ideas off them. And that was all it could be—a *professional* relationship.

Jasper had given up on any other kind of relationship. They never lasted long. Even Dianne, who had at least half a brain, had ended up being only interested in him for what he could spend on her. She'd used him and lied to him like all the others. After he'd sent her packing, he realized his appetite for women had soured. He'd taken off on a long trip after that, one that Edward had disapproved of, saying he was being irresponsible and "running away" from his troubles just as he always did. Just as he had after his mother had died.

After that, he'd stopped partying and dating and buckled down to focus on business a year ago, a decision that had gained approval from his domineering father.

It had been easy to ignore the women who'd thrown themselves at him since. He simply wasn't interested. Or when he did want female companionship, he made sure to put himself first, dating just for what he could get out of it and then discarding them when they got too clingy.

Marly's unique scent—a mixture of vanilla and lemon —remained in the elevator, and Jasper took a deep breath then collapsed into a fit of sneezing. Citrus always did that to him. Citrus or the inkling of a good idea. His mother had always said that his nose was like a barometer for ideas. Whenever he had a sneezing fit at the suggestion of an idea or a new clothing design, it was a sure sign he should not let the idea slip away.

Many years of following that advice had proven his mother right. A pang of loneliness clutched his heart at thoughts of his mom. He missed working closely with her. She'd been the one woman in his life that liked him for him and not his money or status.

Maybe the sneezing had more to do with Marly's ideas than the lemon scent that clung to her. That was a good sign that his instincts to have her work up a plan were spot on. He glanced up toward the heavens, seeking some sort of sign from his mom. Nothing came. Maybe the sneezing was sign enough in itself.

But unless he wanted to carry a box of tissues around, he'd have to remember not to get too close to Marly. He'd have to ignore the pull of those amber eyes and the way her thick mink-brown hair practically begged for him to wrap a finger around one of the silky corkscrew tendrils. No problem there—he wasn't interested, and besides, Marly was his employee. Strictly off-limits.

Not only would it be against company policy, but his father would be pissed. And when his father was pissed at him, he made Jasper's life miserable.

Thoughts of his father made his blood boil. The old man was so rigid in his ways, so controlling. Jasper always felt as if he were still five years old in his father's presence, and he hated that. His mother had always tempered that feeling when she'd been alive, but after her death, things had seemed to only get worse between Jasper and his father.

The elevator doors opened, startling him out of his daydream. He marched out, feeling as if everyone was staring at him. Which, of course, they were, but not because they knew what he was thinking. It was just par for the course when you were the CEO.

He proceeded down the hallway, nodding hello to several employees who passed him but not stopping to talk to them. He'd learned from his father that it usually wasn't a good idea to get too friendly with the employees. As he entered the gym for his daily five p.m. workout, he noticed it was nearly empty. Good. He liked it that way. Better to focus on his workout than have to make small talk.

3

It was seven thirty when Marly finished up her reports for Jasper. She hadn't intended on working that late, but the time flew by. She loved working with sales figures and analyzing the data. Too bad she wouldn't be here long enough to make a career out of it. Still, her personal code of ethics would not allow her to do anything but the best job she could do.

Once she had everything printed out, she realized she had no clue how to get the information to him. She didn't have access to the twentieth floor. She sighed heavily. She would have to call Veronica. She fumbled around for the company directory, locating Veronica's extension. Jasper's wasn't in the directory, which she was kind of thankful for—she didn't know if she would have had the guts to call him directly. She dialed the extension, but it went straight to voicemail. Great. Now what? She was about to start panicking, when her office phone rang.

"Hello? Umm … Marly West speaking." She fumbled her way through.

"Marly, it's Jasper Kenney. Veronica left already for the day, and I figured you might not be able to get in touch with me."

Relief flooded through her. "Oh, yes, I actually just called her. I have everything ready for you."

"I'll send my junior assistant, Sarah, down to get you," Jasper said and hung up.

Marly had no idea who Sarah was, but she hadn't worked at Draconia for long, and as long as she didn't have to deal with Veronica, she was happy. She just hoped Sarah had a better demeanor than Ms. St. James.

A few minutes later, an average-looking girl stepped into her cubicle. She couldn't have been more than twenty-five years old. She grinned sheepishly at her and stuck out her hand.

"Marly? I'm Sarah Thomas. Mr. Kenney sent me to bring you up to his office." She shook her hand firmly. "Oh, I love this jacket!" Sarah said, referring to the jacket that Veronica had made fun of earlier. Was she joking or being sincere? She seemed sincere.

"Thanks. Do you always work so late?" Did Kenney work his assistants like dogs? Would he expect the same hours from her? Marly sensed that Sarah was friendlier than the number-one assistant, and the truth was she could use some friendly conversation.

"Yes. Usually, I am here until ten or eleven, whatever time Mr. Kenney leaves. It doesn't bother me, though. I don't start until three p.m., and it's quiet after six, usually, so I don't have to deal with too much drama. I'm still in school, so I use the time to study." Sarah held the elevator door for Marly and then inserted her card key and pressed the E button for the executive level.

Marly was surprised that Jasper would pay someone to sit around and study. She was also surprised at the difference between Sarah and Veronica St. James. Veronica was always dressed in designer clothes, wore a lot of makeup, and hardly ever cracked a smile. Sarah was noticeably different, wearing slacks, a blouse, and flat shoes. She wore minimal makeup, and her ash-blond hair—natural, not bleached like Veronica's—was long and pulled back loosely with a clip. She was pretty and approachable. Marly instantly liked her.

"Technically, my job is just to make sure Mr. Kenney gets his dinner and that his personal needs are taken care of. Veronica is really his main go-to person for business, but she would never belittle herself to doing things like running to the store to buy his energy drinks." Sarah rolled her eyes and let out a chuckle then grimaced. "Sorry. I shouldn't talk like that."

Marly laughed. "Don't worry. Between you and me, she isn't my favorite person around here."

"Anyway, I guess I'm kind of like a Girl Friday for Mr. Kenney and do all sorts of things. I don't mind. He's been good to my family." Sarah pressed her lips together as if she'd said too much, and Marly didn't dare ask what she'd meant. Then the elevator doors opened, and Sarah put her hand out to hold the doors and let Marly out first.

"Well, here we are," Sarah said.

Marly gasped. The view was breathtaking. The building was situated in downtown New York, and the executive floor was at the top of the building. There were floor-to-ceiling windows, and the lights of the city below sparkled like diamonds.

"Pretty cool, huh? My desk is way over there. Mr. Kenney's office is over here." Sarah started walking in the opposite direction from her desk toward Jasper's office.

Marly followed Sarah down a hallway toward the left. She opened up a set of double doors into the largest office Marly had ever seen. The office exuded power, from the humungous limestone fireplace to the large outdoor patio, complete with a dark-brown rattan-wicker patio set and a matching table and chairs with vibrant red cushions. Inside the office, the furniture was all red mahogany and black leather. There was a desk that had at least six computer screens on it. Jasper stood up from behind the desk.

"Thanks, Sarah. Welcome, Marly. Please take a seat." Jasper gestured toward the large leather chair across from his desk. Marly sat down, taking it all in.

Jasper wasn't wearing his suit. He had on jeans and a regular T-shirt. Marly couldn't help but notice his chest and biceps were extremely solid as the T-shirt was a bit tight on him in those areas. He looked like one of the models that she often toggled in the men's clothing magazines she studied for work. He was tanned and tall, and he had a strong jawline. He also had dimples that showed when he smiled. But even though Jasper looked like a regular guy, Marly reminded herself not to get too comfortable. He was a hardened businessman.

"Do you want anything to drink, or to eat?" Jasper asked as he sat down and pressed a button that made the monitors disappear into his desk.

"No, thank you," Marly replied, wishing she could have a shot of vodka. Why was she so nervous around him?

Jasper nodded to Sarah, and Sarah left the room.

"Okay. Well, show me what you've come up with. I've been looking forward to it all day," Jasper said.

Marly's excitement about her work overshadowed her nerves as she showed him the spreadsheets and explained how she came to the revised sales forecasts and changes in pricing structure she thought they should do. Then, she showed him some ideas she had for the next line, which would be for fall. She had tied everything into the fall line, which she had no access to but needed badly. This was her way in. She needed access to all the designs for that fall lineup.

But aside from that, designing was her true passion. She'd loved coming up with the designs, and the time slipped away as she went over each piece along with the pricing and rollout strategy. And she was good at it. She'd never been good at much in her life. A lifetime of being teased in school for her weight had squelched any self-confidence early on. She was just starting to gain that confidence in her career—too bad it was going to all be for nothing.

Jasper sat back in his chair, steepling his fingers as he studied the information Marly had laid out on his desk.

"Marly, this is pretty impressive. You're going to piss off most of the department heads with this, though. You realize that, right?" Jasper asked.

Marly held eye contact with him. She knew he was challenging her. And it almost seemed a little bit as though he was flirting with her. Then again, he probably flirted with everyone. Probably got his way, too. But that wouldn't happen with her. Marly wasn't going to be a notch on anyone's bedpost, and anyway, she had bigger fish to fry.

Don't look away, she told herself. *You can do this.*

"Well, Mr. Kenney, I'm not doing this to piss anyone off. I'm doing it to help this company increase sales." She couldn't believe she had said the word piss to him.

Jasper's eyes drifted from her face downward. She remembered the stain on her lapel. Ugh. She made a mental note to keep some stain remover in her desk. She self-consciously grabbed at her jacket, pulling it closer together, which only made her breasts bunch out over the top of her bra. Her cheeks warmed, and she wished she was at home on her own couch with a pint of Ben & Jerry's.

Jasper glanced back to the designs. His brow was slightly creased and his mouth pensive, as if he was trying to decide something. Then he sneezed, and his eyes cleared, the ghost of a smile tugging at the corner of his lips as he glanced at a mahogany-framed photograph of an attractive middle-aged woman on the credenza.

"I like the direction you are going with this. Effective immediately, I want you on this project full time. You will also give an update alongside everyone else at the weekly department meeting." Jasper's voice was confident. The voice of a CEO who never had his instructions questioned. He stood up, reaching for a black jacket that was on a very expensive-looking gold coat rack.

"Umm...thanks," Marly sputtered, not sure what to say. This was a huge responsibility. A dream job, really. But her initial reaction was to scream *NO*. She hadn't wanted any recognition, but she knew she could do this, and it would also help her get what she needed for Tanner.

Obviously, she was being dismissed, so she stood up, happy to leave.

"You're welcome. It's late, so why don't I walk you to your car?" Jasper's words shocked her, and she almost tripped.

Hell no.

"Oh, no, that's okay. I walk home late all the time." Marly tried to keep the high-pitched panic tone out of her voice. The last thing she wanted was to spend any more time than possible with him.

Jasper leveled her with a look. "I will give you a ride. This is New York, after all."

And then he smiled, a disarming, crooked smile that revealed perfect white teeth. Jasper kept his distance from her as they walked toward the elevator. Marly desperately looked around for Sarah, hoping she would emerge, but she didn't.

"No, really, I don't want you to have to go to any trouble, Mr. Kenney." The thought of getting into his car with him was giving her heart palpitations. She had heard he was a heartless jerk. Why would he care if she walked home alone? Oh wait... Was he trying to put the moves on her?

"Marly, call me Jasper, please. And I insist on giving you a ride. It isn't up for debate," Jasper said firmly.

"Okay, if you insist. I just need to grab my purse first." The guy was insistent, and he was used to getting his way. Better to just let him give her a ride than to argue with him. Arguing might seem suspicious, and that was the last thing she wanted.

The elevator doors opened up at Marly's floor, and Jasper held them for her to exit. He jumped back as she brushed past him. "I'll get my car and meet you out front."

Marly ran to her cubicle and grabbed her purse then headed back toward the elevator. Pressing the G button, she realized she had no idea how she would know which car was Jasper's. Since this was New York City, the front of the building was on a main street. Taxis stopped there all the time, and cars would double park there, but how was she going to know which one was his, especially as it was dark out?

She stepped out of the elevator, her heels clicking as she walked across the huge marble lobby to the main doors. She said good night to the security guard, and he buzzed her out.

The cool air felt good on her face as she stepped outside. She instantly went from the cool quietness of the office to the hustle and bustle of the warm, humid city streets filled with the smell of diesel and the sound of horns honking and people yelling.

She was hesitantly walking down the large steps that led to the street when a red car pulled up. She wasn't sure what kind it was, but it was the shiniest vehicle she had ever seen. The windows were tinted black, and she couldn't see inside. Her instincts told her it was Jasper. She approached slowly as the driver's-side door opened and Jasper emerged, crossing in front of the car to the passenger side.

"Allow me." He opened the door for Marly, and she slid inside, sinking into the buttery-soft leather, which cradled her as if it were custom made for her body. The car was a perfect seventy-eight degrees and had that pleasant new-car smell that Marly always loved.

"So where are we headed?" Jasper asked her as he slowly weaved in and out of traffic. Even though it was nine p.m., the streets were full, as usual.

"West Easton Street," Marly said, amazed at how smooth the car rode. "This car is gorgeous," she commented, almost to herself.

"Thanks. I know it isn't practical to have a car in the city, especially when I live next door to where I work." Jasper chuckled as he said this. "I just like to drive. It takes my mind off of things."

"I've never had a car. I grew up in the city and just never really needed one. But when it's snowing or raining out, I sure wish I did." Marly hoped she didn't sound stupid.

"Well, it looks like we have something in common. I grew up in the city, too, and this is my first car. I never had one before this." Jasper slowed down, as traffic was almost at a standstill up ahead due to the ever-constant night construction in the city.

Marly relaxed a tad. Jasper didn't seem as if he was trying to put the moves on her, and he was actually kind of nice. She smiled at the thought of her and Jasper Kenney having something in common. He probably had chauffeured limousines his whole life, and she had been lucky to have money to take the subway.

She wondered where he had grown up. Probably some giant penthouse on Park Avenue. She'd grown up in a townhouse, which was actually very nice, but was probably the size of Jasper's bathroom. Her father had owned his own plumbing company and worked long hours to provide for his family, which was probably what led to his heart attack five years ago. Marly had always felt guilty about that.

Jasper turned the car down West Easton Street.

"It's in the middle. You can pull over anywhere," Marly said, eager to get out even though the ride hadn't been awkward as she'd envisioned. Thank God she lived so close to work.

Jasper pulled the car over, and before Marly knew it, he had jumped out and was opening her door for her. He extended his hand, and she instinctively reached for it. She tried to act smooth as she stepped out, but with her being the klutz that she was, her heel missed the curb and she fell back, prompting Jasper to pull on her hand.

She stumbled against him, feeling hard muscles and smelling the spicy scent of aftershave.

She pushed away from him and stumbled onto the sidewalk.

"Sorry about that. My car isn't the best curbside. It's so low." Jasper's voice was husky.

Marly tried to keep her tone light. "No worries. It's such a gorgeous car. Thanks again for the ride. I'll see you tomorrow, Mr. Kenney."

"You're welcome. Good work today!"

She thought she heard him sneeze as she practically ran down the sidewalk to her townhouse, her pulse skittering like a frightened rabbit's.

She heard the light toot of his car horn and turned around in time to see him wave as his car sped by. A feeling of giddiness bubbled up inside her. Jasper Kenney liked her work!

But the small sliver of happiness she allowed herself to feel was crushed when she reached her door and saw a notice on it. She ripped it off, her hands trembling as she read it.

Foreclosure.

It was from the bank. She crumpled it up, throwing it down in the foyer as she walked inside. For the second time that day, tears threatened, and this time she let them fall.

There wasn't much of a mortgage left, but after her father died, she and her mother had struggled to make the payments. They had managed until last year, when everything had started to happen.

She headed upstairs, wiping the salty tears from her cheeks. Any career-advancement thoughts she'd entertained soured. She couldn't risk getting in deeper than she already was, not when she was closer than ever to being able to fix all her problems.

JASPER WATCHED MARLY in the rearview mirror as he pulled out into traffic. His mother had raised him to be a gentleman, so he'd offered to give her a ride. His father would probably admonish him for spending time with one of the worker-bees, but Marly was a nice kid. Well, not really a kid, as he guessed she was in her late twenties —not that much younger than him—but she was still fairly new in fashion design.

She didn't exactly dress the part, though, he thought as he watched her walk into her building. Maybe they weren't paying her enough. His gaze drifted from her somewhat outdated suit and lingered on her calves, which were made even more shapely by her high heels.

Honk!

Jasper jerked his head forward, his quick reflexes saving him from smashing into the car coming up on his left.

What the hell was he thinking?

Jasper shook his head, picturing the sour look on his father's face if he knew that Jasper had almost smashed up the Ferrari because he was looking at a mere woman.

Heck, even though Jasper wasn't interested in a relation-ship, he could still look.

Thing was, he liked Marly. She wasn't stuck up or pretentious. She didn't try to put the moves on him or seem at all interested in his money. Not to mention her idea for the clothing line was spot on. And she had a sweetness about her, which could be a disadvantage. Marly was out of her league pitted against the sharks in the sales office at Draconia. She'd have to watch her back —or maybe he would have to watch it for her.

He glanced back one more time as she disappeared through her door. A feeling of protectiveness washed over him, and his eyes automatically scanned the side-walk to make sure no one was following her. New York City could be a dangerous place, and he didn't like the thought of any harm coming to her.

The traffic eased up, and he pushed down the gas pedal, feeling the hum of the motor as his sweaty palm shifted gears.

Pushing the car harder, he headed toward the high-way, planning to run the car as fast as he could.

4

The next morning, Jasper stepped off the elevator and was immediately met by Veronica St. James.

"Mr. Kenney, Mr. Henderson and Mr. Quirk would like to meet with you as soon as possible. You do have an opening at eight thirty. It's regarding Miss West, I believe." Veronica sneered as she said "Miss West." "You know, the girl who—"

"I know who she is." Jasper cut her off a little more sharply than he had intended. Veronica had worked for him for years, and while she was extremely efficient at her job, he did not like her penchant for drama. Plus, he got the feeling she wanted more than an employer-employee relationship, and he was not in the least bit interested. "Send them up now."

Veronica turned and sashayed to her desk, calling the two department heads and telling them they could meet with Jasper now.

Jasper looked across his desk at Bill Henderson, VP of

Sales, and Steve Quirk, VP of Marketing. They had come to ask why Marly West was given access to their departments' files. They weren't happy about it.

"I understand your concerns. Ms. West is working on a special project, directly for me. I authorized her access. She will be presenting at the weekly meetings, effective immediately, and at that time I'm sure you will understand why," he said dryly. He didn't like to be questioned, and certainly not about something that was the result of these two individuals dropping the ball in their areas. Lack of sales wasn't acceptable.

Bill and Steve looked at each other.

"Jasper, our main concern is her background, her experience. I mean, she's fairly new in the fashion industry. She's only been here a month, and let's face it, she doesn't exactly scream 'style.'" Bill Henderson was always the most outspoken one in the room. Jasper liked that about him. Usually.

Jasper frowned. "What does that mean? *Style?*"

Steve chimed in. "Jasper, she sticks out like a sore thumb here."

Jasper's blood boiled, not only in defense of Marly, but also in defense of his company. Was that what his VPs thought was important? Looks? No wonder sales were slipping. Then again, wasn't this what his father had always drilled into them? Into *him*?

Jasper stood up, looking down at the two men. Maybe his father's outdated ideas were dragging the company down.

"And why is that?" he demanded. "Because she isn't an

emaciated Barbie doll? Because she doesn't wear the same designers the other women in this office do, even though most of them probably aren't able to pay their rent because they are paying a thousand dollars for a pair of shoes?

"You two are both at least twenty pounds overweight. Do you realize that? This company doesn't just run on the looks of people. It runs on the ability of the senior executives to create, evaluate, and implement what is necessary to maintain Draconia's lead in the fashion industry.

"You two dropped the ball with the new line. The fact that someone who has minimal experience in this industry was able to figure that out should embarrass you." Jasper spoke in clipped, even tones, reining himself in so as to refrain from yelling at the two men.

Bill and Steve's faces turned red. They nodded in silence, knowing better than to argue with Jasper when he was like this. Without a further word, they stood and left.

Jasper looked out his window. He *had* given Marly a lot of responsibility. And it wasn't like him to take on a new person, an unknown, and bring them into the circles of upper management. No wonder Steve and Bill were so shocked.

A seed of doubt took root in his stomach. Had he given that assignment to Marly because of her abilities, or was there another reason? Why had he defended her like that in the meeting?

For the first time ever, he questioned his judgment.

No, he had done the right thing. Marly had brought data to light that the others had ignored … or hidden. Draconia's sales had been dwindling, and Marly did have good points and a great perspective, something that no one else had brought to the table.

He glanced at the mahogany-framed photo of his mother that sat on the credenza. She'd died twelve years ago, but he could still feel her influence. Still feel her comforting presence. Still smell her gardenia-scented perfume. His early decisions had been guided by doing what his mother would think was right. Jasper was startled to realize that he'd gotten away from that recently, especially since he'd taken over the company. Was he turning into a carbon copy of his father?

His mother had been smart and sweet. The complete opposite of his father. His mother had taught him to value people for what was on the inside, not how they looked. His father was more interested in appearances, and clearly that attitude had rubbed off on the Draconia executive team. But Jasper hadn't done much to change that since he'd taken over. Maybe now was the time.

He couldn't believe Bill and Steve's remarks about Marly's appearance. What did that have to do with her skills on the job? Besides, Jasper thought she looked fine. Healthy. In fact, he preferred her look to the skinny women that his father liked to hire.

Thoughts of his father made his stomach clench. Edward felt that anyone who wore over a size four was fat, which was ridiculous, but Jasper would never have the courage to tell him that. His father had built an empire based on that way of thinking. He had also gone through three wives, all who seemed more interested in his money than an actual marriage.

Jasper hadn't had much luck in that department, either. He had never married and had never had a serious relationship, as the women all seemed drawn to his money. He typically had a girlfriend for a few weeks, and then he would dump her and move on to the next.

Jasper leaned back in his chair and smiled at the thought of the stodgy old men's club that made up the Draconia executive team being bested by a woman. Draconia had been, for the most part, a man's company all these years. They had never even had a woman on the senior executive team. It wasn't because he was against it —it was that no one had ever been aggressive enough to earn a spot. The women all seemed to be too busy competing in the fashion area to move ahead in their careers. He felt Marly West might be a game-changer. He hoped his instincts were right. Otherwise, he was going to be eating a lot of crow.

5

Tanner Durcotte paced back and forth in his office. He hadn't heard from Marly in a few days. Not acceptable. She should know better—he wasn't a patient man. Fall was fast approaching, and he was under the gun at Theorim to increase sales, somehow. His phone rang, and he picked it up immediately.

"Where have you been? You need to keep me updated daily, Marly. Every day," Tanner almost yelled to her.

"Tanner, calm down. This isn't going to happen overnight. You knew that. Just because you don't hear from me doesn't mean I am not working on the plan. In fact, it's going better than I could have imagined. I expect that within two weeks, I will have something solid for you." Marly's voice was barely above a whisper. She must be at work, where she couldn't talk. So what? Tanner didn't care if she got into trouble except for the fact that he needed her there until she got him what he wanted.

"Two weeks?" Tanner screeched. "No. That is too

long, Marly. I need something in one week. No longer. Otherwise, the whole thing is off." He hung up on her abruptly.

MARLY SCOWLED at the phone in her hand. Tanner was impossible to deal with. He was asking for too much, too soon. But she had to figure out how to get it done faster now. Her thought process was interrupted by a cheerful-sounding, "Hi, Marly."

Turning around, she saw Sarah Thomas.

"Oh, hi, Sarah! Happy Monday." Marly grinned.

"Ugh. I hate Mondays. Did you have a good weekend? I spent mine studying. Not much fun." Sarah rambled on as they both walked toward the elevators.

"I spent mine working, so I guess we are even. What are you studying, anyway?" Marly asked her. Sarah was too old to be a full-time college student, unless she was going for her master's or studying to be a lawyer or something.

"Food! Well, I already have a degree in finance. I spent some time in the field and hated it. Then I switched to fashion, but that didn't take either. But I've always loved food, love to cook, so I decided that was my real calling. My parents weren't happy with all my career changes, but oh well. I'm paying for it myself. So the studying is actually cooking and learning about different methods, et cetera. It's pretty cool," Sarah explained to Marly, her smile cheerful. Marly really liked her—she was so down to earth.

The elevator stopped at Marly's floor. "Well, here's my stop. I'll talk to you later."

"Okay. Maybe we can do lunch later on. I'm in early all this week and not used to having to fend for myself for lunch," Sarah said, laughing as the doors closed shut.

Marly walked to her cube, smiling. Sarah was the first person who had actually tried to have a conversation with her since she had been here. It felt good.

Her mind wandered back to Tanner, and she realized she needed to work on that issue. And fast. She sat at her computer and accessed the server that had the company's couture designs on it. There was a file that contained the designs that had been rejected for previous years. She had an idea. She picked up her phone and texted Tanner.

"Meet me at Café Lazure at eight tonight." She glanced around to make sure no one could see what she was doing and started to implement her idea.

WHEN MARLY GOT to Café Lazure later that night, Tanner was already seated, with what looked like a vodka tonic in front of him. She paused in the door, her mouth curling up in disgust as she looked at the back of his balding head. She hated having to deal with him, but there was no other way.

How had things gotten so far out of hand? Tanner and his wife, Emily, had been close family friends. Or so she'd thought. Marly's heart sunk as she remembered her mother sitting at Emily's bedside while she had chemotherapy. Cooking meals for Tanner. Tanner had been nice back then, like a kind old uncle. But after Emily died, Tanner had turned mean. And when Marly's mother had needed help, Tanner had offered, and Marly had had no choice but to accept.

She walked to the table, a large manila folder clutched in her hand. She slid into a chair across from Tanner and ordered a glass of white wine from the waitress.

"I am still working on it. But since you insisted on getting started, I brought these. I think they will help you get on your way." Marly pushed papers across the table to him. There were four pages of designs, with information on all the materials, estimated revenue, everything.

Tanner's beady eyes lit up as he looked through them.

"Excellent. Excellent. Wait. These are dated three years ago. What's up with that?"

Marly's heart lurched. She was hoping he wouldn't notice the date. She told herself not to panic. She hadn't been able to alter the designs in any way, due to her access level. She knew the dates on it were three years old. She was ready for this question.

"They've been working on the designs for three years, Tanner. That's how good these are. They were waiting to roll out the line for a specific price point and consumer—young women. So that's why other lines were released before this." Hopefully she sounded convincing enough that Tanner bought it.

Tanner's narrowed eyes flicked from her to the

papers and back again. He sat back in his chair. "I guess that makes sense. I don't know. These look kind of shitty, though. Don't you think? Then again, most of what passes for 'fashion' these days looks like crap. And I am not good with women's designs, anyway. But I need a lot more than these. This is just four designs."

"I know, Tanner. I got what I could right now since you seemed so insistent that you have something right away." Marly tried not to sound irritated. She didn't want Tanner to get angry. "It's going to take me a lot longer to get the full line."

"Okay, okay. I guess this is better than nothing. But I expect everything in the next week. Got it?" Tanner picked up the menu.

"Got it," Marly said.

How in the hell was she going to pull this off? She still had her presentation due at the management meeting in two days and her regular work to get done. The last thing she needed was to get fired or have anyone monitoring her work.

They both ordered a light meal, and Marly suffered through small talk during dinner. She would rather have been anywhere else, but Tanner was an old family friend, and she didn't need him mentioning anything to her mother about her being rude.

Finally, they were done with the meal and the waitress appeared at the table.

"Dessert?" she asked as she scooped up their dinner plates.

"None for me, thanks," Tanner replied, throwing his napkin on the table.

"Me, either. Thank you." Marly really did want dessert. Making small talk with Tanner was stressful, and dessert always helped. But she had decided she would try and cut out sweets for a while. After losing the fifty pounds, she wanted to keep the momentum going and lose twenty more. Working with a bunch of stick figures made it somewhat easy to turn down dessert.

The waitress left the bill on the table, and Tanner grabbed it, throwing some money down. He stood up. "I'll be in touch, Marly. Good job so far." And with that, he walked out of the restaurant.

Relief flooded through Marly as she watched him leave. She couldn't believe she had gotten away with what she had done. Those designs were horrible, but Tanner himself had admitted he had no fashion sense. That had always come from Emily. Why Tanner kept up the fashion company after her death instead of selling was a mystery to Marly. Maybe the small restaurants he also owned didn't bring in enough money. Or maybe he was just greedy. Or maybe he needed to fill his time with Emily gone.

At first, she had felt kind of bad deceiving him, but then smartened up. Tanner wasn't her friend. If he wanted to help her, he could have done it without asking her to risk her job and betray her company.

Her chest constricted as she thought about Jasper. She had to admit that she kind of liked the guy. He'd put his confidence in her, which made stealing the designs even more repulsive. But at the same time, she owed him nothing and owed her family everything. If it was just the foreclosure, that would be one thing, but Marly had a more urgent reason to have to play ball with the likes of Tanner Durcotte.

Besides, the warm, fuzzy feelings she had about Jasper were just fantasies. She knew she was just some girl in sales. She'd never be the next VP of sales at Draconia... or anything else to him. Which was good because if she was more than that, she might not be able to follow through with what Tanner wanted. And she knew she would have to do that sooner rather than later—Tanner would not be placated by the designs she'd given him tonight for very long.

VERONICA ST. JAMES was not in a good mood as she walked the crowded New York streets toward home. She hadn't had the best day at work, starting with Jasper snapping at her. To make matters worse, he had ignored her the rest of the day, handing off work to Sarah instead. He had even asked Sarah to come in early all week. The nerve!

Veronica was the best thing that could happen to Jasper—he just didn't realize that yet. And she didn't just mean in the office, either. Veronica had had her sights on Jasper for years now, and she'd made major sacrifices to get the job as his assistant—the first step in her plan to become Mrs. Jasper Kenney. But now, it seemed that was all going to shit. And she had a feeling it had something to do with that new bitch, Marly West.

She glanced into the window of Café Lazure as she passed, her heart skidding to a stop. She slowed down then stopped. She walked by again just to make sure she was seeing things correctly. She was.

Marly West was having dinner with Tanner Durcotte, the CEO of Theorim Fashion House. What the hell? As she continued to walk by, her mind raced.

How the hell would Marly even know Tanner? And why would they be having dinner?

There was no way they could be a couple. Marly was too frumpy, and everyone in the industry knew that after Tanner's wife had passed away, he had focused one hundred percent on the company, and never dated or even went out with women. Veronica was blown away.

She ducked behind a pillar so she could spy on them unnoticed. She couldn't tell exactly what they were saying, but just the fact that they were together had alarm bells sounding in her head.

Suddenly, the day was improving. Taking her cell phone out, she snapped off a few photos. This was an interesting development. Veronica saw it as proof that her instincts about Marly were right. Marly was up to something, and she'd have to watch her very closely. Sooner or later, she would screw up, and Veronica would be there to catch her.

6

J asper stepped off the elevator and headed toward his office. It was six a.m. Veronica wouldn't be in for another hour, and he was starving. He didn't have much food at his place. He emailed Sarah and asked if she could stock his house with some food later. He trusted Sarah more than Veronica when it came to those types of things. Veronica felt it was beneath her to do that, and besides, Sarah was an awesome cook.

"Well, looks like you take after your old man, huh?" Edward Kenney walked into Jasper's office, referring to the time. Jasper's father had always started work at six a.m. No exceptions. Jasper had thought he was nuts when he was growing up, yet as soon as he started working, he found himself doing the same thing. He liked to get a jump on the day.

"Unfortunately. Good to see you, Dad." Jasper clasped his father's hand for a formal handshake. There was not much hugging between the two. Why was Edward here? He usually only showed up when there was a problem and for the annual stockholder meetings.

"It makes me proud to see you take after me, son. I never question if the company is in good hands with you at the helm." Edward's uncustomary praise set Jasper on edge.

Edward walked over to the windows, taking in the magnificent views. "I always did love this view."

"Yes. You did a great job picking out the office space, that's for sure," Jasper said. When he was a little boy, he had loved visiting his father at the office, even though Edward was usually too busy to spend any time with him.

Jasper would look out the window, and Edward's then-secretary, Mary, would point out things to him and then take him to her desk, where she always had candy for him. When Mary died several years ago, it was one of the few times Jasper and his father had hugged.

Mary had worked for Edward for forty years and had been like a second mother to Jasper. Especially during the times when Jasper's own mother was ill and confined to bed—which had been many times off and on during Jasper's childhood.

Both Jasper and Edward had been crushed when Mary had passed away. Odd for Edward since he tended to treat all the employees like pieces of furniture, but not Mary. Jasper couldn't picture ever having the same relationship with Veronica that Edward had had with Mary.

"So how are things, anyway? I've heard there's a new gal around here," Edward asked as he sat down on the plush leather couch across from the fireplace. So *that* was the real reason for Edward's visit.

"Things are good. A new gal? Well, there is a woman, Marly West, who has brought some new insight into things, and I have her working on a project for me, if that's who you mean."

Jasper knew it was. Bill or Steve, or both, must have called his father to tell him what was going on. Both of them had been hired by Edward years ago, and Jasper had kept them on more out of loyalty than anything. He hadn't been thrilled with them the past few years, but he was always able to count on the managers under them to excel in their departments, so he had left it as is.

Edward nodded. "Well, I'm sure you have it under control. I just wouldn't want you to be thinking with other parts of your body when making these types of decisions."

Jasper bit his tongue. Did his father think he was that irresponsible? He knew better than to say anything. He wasn't going to argue about it.

"I have everything under control. Don't let the panic calls worry you." Jasper would certainly remember that someone had made a call to his father. He hoped he could figure out who. He expected loyalty, regardless of whether or not the person was hired by his father. Jasper ran the company now, not Edward. But as soon as Jasper had that thought, he knew that he wouldn't do much of anything. For some reason, going against his father still terrified him, and it was easier to let things go on as they were.

"I know you do, son," Edward said as he stood up, smiling. "You know this company will always be my baby. Let's go grab some breakfast."

Jasper really didn't want to spend the time to eat breakfast with Edward, but he knew better than to refuse his father. Besides, he was starving. He just hoped that he could keep the conversation steered toward mundane company matters and away from Marly West.

VERONICA TAPPED A PERFECTLY manicured nail on the smooth steel railing inside the elevator as she waited for it to make its way to her floor.

"Hurry up, for crying out loud." She glanced at her watch. Six fifteen. She'd never been in this early before, but today she had important work to do.

The doors whooshed opened, and she almost jumped out of her designer heels when she saw Jasper and Edward Kenney standing there.

"Hello, Veronica. You're looking as beautiful as ever," Edward said, eyeballing her up and down. Veronica wished Jasper had the same dirty thoughts in his head about her as she was sure his father did.

She sidestepped out of the elevator as they entered, purposely brushing her small breasts against Jasper's arm. She looked up at him, only to see a sour expression on his face.

Jasper's brows ticked up. "In early, Veronica?"

"Yes, I have some work I wanted to catch up on," she lied. Let him think she was putting in extra time for the company. It would make her seem that much more valuable.

"Oh. Good." Jasper seemed surprised. "I'll be down in the café with my father if anyone needs me."

The elevator closed, and Veronica rushed over to her desk. She logged onto her computer and then onto Marly's PC. No one knew she had full access to everyone's computer, as well as all the servers, aside from Jasper.

It had been given to her years ago in case of an emergency, which had happened when Jasper was traveling and couldn't get in remotely. She never used it aside from when Jasper asked her to, which was always for accessing reports. She probably shouldn't be using it now, but she was sure the results would justify her actions.

She scrolled through Marly's files, not seeing anything out of place. Then she noticed something titled 2014.

Why would Marly have anything from 2014? She hadn't even worked there then. Veronica opened the file. It was rejected designs for the company's 2014 fall line. What the hell? Probably something she needed for the stupid report Jasper had asked her to do.

But wait. She'd seen paperwork on the table in between Marly and Tanner last night. Had Marly shared designs with him? What would be the point of sharing the crappy, rejected designs from years ago? She didn't know, but this was something she would definitely file away for future use. She took screenshots of the files and tucked them away inside a folder, keeping them ready until she knew exactly how to use them to her advantage.

7

Marly was waiting for a group of people to exit the elevator in Draconia's lobby when the one next to her pinged opened. Inside, she saw Jasper Kenney with an older, distinguished-looking gentleman. She could tell by the chiseled looks of the older man that he must be Edward Kenney, Jasper's father.

They were deep in conversation, and neither one of them noticed her. Good. That was what she wanted to be. Unnoticeable.

She boarded the elevator and saw them head toward the cafeteria just before the doors closed. The cafeteria reminded her of food, and she made a mental note to ask Sarah to go to lunch, as she hadn't been able to the day before and had felt guilty about it. She proceeded to her desk and turned her computer on, ready to start work.

Several hours passed, and she realized it was eleven thirty. She picked up her phone and dialed Sarah's extension.

"Hey, stranger!" Sarah answered in her usual cheery voice.

"Hi. I wanted to see if you wanted to do lunch today." Marly's stomach grumbled as if to punctuate the question.

"Well, I would, but I brought some of my latest creations in. Why don't you come up here and sample them? I'm always looking for feedback. God knows I can't ask Veronica. She doesn't eat." Sarah giggled as she said the last sentence.

Marly burst into laughter. "That sounds great. But are you sure I should come up there?" She didn't want Jasper to be angry if she started to become friendly with his assistant.

"Of course. I'll come get you," Sarah replied and hung up before Marly could say anything.

Marly headed toward the elevators, and in a few seconds, the doors opened, and Sarah gestured her inside, pressing E on the panel.

The elevator glided up to the top floor then stopped.

"I know Jasper needs security, but this whole card-access-only thing is a pain in my butt!" Sarah said as she slid her employee badge into a slot under the keypad and entered a code. 7842. Marly's heartbeat quickened, and a pang of guilt shot through her as she memorized the numbers. She wasn't sure if the key code would work with her card, but if it did, this could be her way to get the access she needed to satisfy Tanner and be done with him once and for all.

The doors slid open, and they stepped off the elevator. Marly followed Sarah to her desk, which was not near Veronica's—phew!—and was in a large alcove with a great view. Sarah took several dishes out of her full-size refrigerator and popped one into the microwave.

"I hope you like garlic," Sarah said, taking the dish out of the microwave and handing it Marly. It smelled amazing.

"I love it!" Marly tried not to drool at the tangy smell of the garlic mixed with something more savory. She grabbed a fork and used the side to cut off a small piece, and her taste buds tingled with the smooth texture of pasta, coated in creamy garlic sauce and topped with savory rosemary chicken. It was delicious.

"Sarah, this tastes amazing," Marly mumbled around the food stuffed in her mouth.

"You really think so? I made it up last night. I'm big on spices and tend to throw a bit too much in at times," Sarah said. "Here, try some of the bread I made, and there's some cobbler, also." Sarah handed over more dishes.

They ate in silence, Marly relaxing in the comfort of a new friend. She didn't have many of those. Her gut tightened as she remembered how her weight had always made her the odd one out. Never picked for dodgeball. Never invited to parties at school. But she was an adult now. Almost thirty years old. And she was no longer overweight. She let her insecurities slide and enjoyed having lunch with a friend.

Marly was shoving another large forkful of food into her mouth when Jasper's head peeked around the corner.

"I'm headed out for my one thirty meeting, Sarah. I won't be back today. What is that smell?" Jasper's eyes drifted to the dishes lying on the table.

"Oh, I made a few dishes that I'm testing out for my class tonight. I brought in samples. You want some?" Sarah asked.

"They smell great, but I don't have any time." Jasper's voice was laced with disappointment.

Marly stopped eating, feeling self-conscious. She didn't want to be stuffing her face in front of Jasper.

"Okay, but here—take a piece of this rosemary garlic bread I made for the road." Sarah handed Jasper a large piece of bread, which he took with him as he walked away.

"You two seem to have a good relationship. You're at ease with him," Marly said as she finished up her pasta.

"Yeah. Mr. Kenney's a really nice guy. He can be pretty down to earth, also, believe it or not," Sarah replied.

Nice guy? That was not what the word on the street was. But Marly was discovering that the word on the street might not be correct. And she remembered how Sarah had said that Jasper had helped her family. She was dying to know more about it. Did they have a relationship that went beyond employer and employee? Maybe Sarah was an old family friend. Hopefully not like Tanner was an old family friend of Marly's. The thought reminded her that after everyone found out what she had done for Tanner, Sarah would probably hate her. No sense in getting too personal with someone who wouldn't be in her life for very long. Too bad because she was starting to really like Sarah.

They finished up their lunch, and Marly excused herself to go back downstairs and finish up prepping for her presentation the next day.

In the back of her mind, the "project" for Tanner weighed heavily. As the clock ticked away, she grew more and more anxious. By 6:30 p.m., she was finished. She headed toward the elevators, ready to go home.

As the elevator doors shut, she had an idea. She pressed the E button. When the elevator stopped, she put her key card into the slot and then entered "7842" into the keypad.

The doors opened up onto Jasper's floor. Holy crap. It had worked. All the key cards must be the same. It was the code you needed to access this floor!

Marly stepped off the elevator. Her mind was racing. Jasper had said he wouldn't be coming back after lunch, and Sarah was gone to class. Veronica never worked past five p.m.

The floor was dark and quiet. No one else was here.

Marly walked briskly to Jasper's office, reaching out for the metal knob on the door. She held her breath. Would it open? To her amazement, it did. Apparently, Jasper didn't need to lock his door since only people with the code could get to the floor.

She pulled the door open and slipped inside, slowly shutting the door behind her so it didn't make any noise. Her heart thudded against her ribs as she studied the office. Where did he keep the designs?

His office was neat and orderly. Everything in its place and no clutter. For a CEO, he didn't have a lot of places for files.

She walked to the large credenza behind his desk and pulled on one of the drawers.

It was locked.

She tried another.

Also locked.

Dammit!

The fall designs were in his office. Everyone in the company knew he kept them in here, just as his father had done when he was in charge. But she couldn't stay in here long. She had to look quickly … if she were caught in here, there was no telling what would happen. At the very least, she'd be fired, and then how would she get those designs for Tanner?

She glanced nervously at the door. The shades in the window to the hallway were closed, but she could tell it was still dark out there. Still no sign of anyone around. The ticking of the clock echoed loudly in her ears, ratcheting up her anxiety with each passing second.

Her eyes fell on the computer. There were no designs on any of the servers, and she had heard through the grapevine that once a line was completed and approved, only Jasper held the designs until after the runway shows were complete.

She eyed the two built-in cabinets on either side of the fireplace. She yanked on one, and it opened. Too bad —all that was in there was a bunch of bottles of booze and some glasses. High-end stuff, too. But that didn't help her. She was just about to shut it when a sound in the hallway caught her attention.

She froze, her eyes darting to the door.

The knob turned, and the door whooshed open, causing Marly's heart to jerk in her chest.

"Marly? What are you doing in here?"

8

J asper stood in the doorway, frowning at her. Marly's heart raced. She tried to swallow the panic welling up inside her, ignoring the other feeling— the one of guilt or regret—she wasn't sure which—at being caught in the act.

Jasper let the door shut, and it clicked in place. He came further into the office. Closer to her.

"Oh. Hi, Mr. Kenney ... I mean, Jasper. I was just waiting for you, and, err, this is embarrassing, but I wanted a drink, so I was checking if you had anything. I'm sorry." Marly hoped he would buy her lame excuse.

"Waiting for me?" Jasper frowned, and Marly was relieved to see all traces of suspicion disappear from his face. "Did we have a meeting?"

"I thought we did. Didn't you say you wanted to see me before the meeting tomorrow?" Marly asked him, surprised at how fast she was coming up with this BS.

Jasper reached past her to grab a bottle of scotch from

the shelf. His scent wafted over to her—sandalwood and spice—and her stomach did a little flip. She stepped back, reluctantly.

He took the bottle and two glasses to his desk and poured them both a drink.

"I don't think I said that, but with the day I've had, anything is possible. Here." Jasper handed Marly one of the glasses. He sat in the chair and indicated for her to sit on the couch.

"I thought Veronica said you wanted to go over them," Marly said. She felt bad about throwing Veronica under the bus. Sort of. But if Jasper questioned Veronica and she denied telling Marly about the meeting, who would he believe? Oh well, she could probably cover, and in another week or so, it wouldn't matter anyway.

Jasper frowned again. "We must have gotten our wires crossed."

"Oh! Well, I'm sorry. I don't want to waste any of your time," Marly said quickly as she took a swig of scotch and tried not to cough from it. She placed the glass carefully on the green onyx coaster on the coffee table and tried to ignore the burn in her throat while she sprung up, happy to get out of there as fast as possible. "I'll just let you get back to work."

Jasper motioned for her to sit back down. "That's okay. I'd like to know what you've come up with. It's important to the company. Why don't you brief me on what you're presenting tomorrow?"

Now what was she going to do? She didn't have a briefing prepared. She'd have to wing it.

The burn of the scotch had turned into a relaxing warm glow. Maybe another swig would help. She picked the glass up carefully and swilled the rest down.

Jasper raised a brow then tilted the bottle toward her glass. "More?"

The liquid courage was helping. One more sip couldn't hurt. She scooted closer to him and held out her glass.

Jasper started to pour, then he made a funny face. His nose twitched. He put the bottle down, sucked in a breath, and let out the loudest sneeze Marly had ever heard.

Startled, Marly jumped. Her grip loosened on the tumbler full of scotch, and it slipped out of her hand, landing smack-dab in Jasper's lap.

"Oh my God. I'm so sorry! I'm such a klutz! Let me get that." Marly grabbed a bunch of napkins that were on the table, and she instinctively crouched in front of his chair, swiping at the growing stain on his thigh with the napkins.

Jasper grabbed her hands. "No! I mean that's okay. Not your fault. It'll dry."

Marly stared up at him, embarrassed. Had she really just lunged to the floor to wipe the boss's crotch? He probably thought she was trying to hit on him. But instead of the hint of disgust she expected to see in Jasper's eyes, she saw a flicker of something else. Desire? No, must be the scotch. She was just glad he wasn't handing her a pink slip.

"Oh, sorry... I..." Marly didn't know exactly what to say as she still crouched in front of him like a ditz.

Before she could push up from her position, the doorknob rattled. Marly's blood froze as the door started to open, and she heard Veronica's screechy voice.

"Jasper ... are you in there? Your father is on his way up."

Veronica's mouth dropped open as she pushed into the room to see Marly kneeling in front of Jasper's chair. Marly sprung up, tripped backwards over the coffee table, and landed splayed-legged on the couch. Her arms flailed in the air as she struggled to sit upright.

"Oh, err, I didn't know you were busy." Veronica eyed Marly up and down, then her eyes widened as they zoned in on Jasper's wet crotch. Marly's cheeks flamed. It figured Veronica would get the wrong idea. But she had to admit she took a smug satisfaction in the flare of jealousy she saw in Veronica's eyes.

"We were just going over something. I spilled my drink. What do you need?" Jasper's tone reflected a hint of annoyance as he dabbed at his pants with the napkin. He glanced at the green marble clock on the mantle. "What are you doing here at this hour, anyway?"

"Don't you remember? I'm making up hours because I took last Friday off. Anyway, your father is on his way up. I just wanted you to be aware." Veronica gave Marly one last pointed look, turned on her heel, and stomped to her desk.

Marly pushed up from the sofa and headed toward the door. This was the perfect excuse to get out of there before she had to ad-lib an update. Not to mention she was embarrassed about the whole drink-spilling incident.

"Sorry about the spill. I'll update you on the project tomorrow," Marly said.

She kept her eyes glued to the floor as she rushed toward the door, almost running straight into Edward Kenney, who had paused in the doorway.

"Whoa, there. What are you running away from?" Edward said it as a joke, but Marly wished a giant hole would open up and swallow her.

"Edward Kenney, this is Marly West. Marly, this is my father, and the founder of Draconia Fashions, Edward Kenney," Jasper balled up the napkin and tossed it into the trash.

Marly extended her hand to shake Edward's and caught his eyes moving from her head down her body and back up again.

"Nice to meet you, Marly. I've heard a lot about you." Edward's smile was as heart-stopping as Jasper's. They even had the same dimples.

"Nice to meet you, too, Mr. Kenney." Marly backed out the door, managing to avoid looking at Jasper. "Okay, I'll update you tomorrow, Mr. Kenney." She waved loosely in Jasper's direction. "Sorry about the... umm... accident."

She hurried out into the hall, fighting the urge to run and ignoring the daggers Veronica was shooting into her back with eyes. She forced herself to slowly walk to the elevator and calmly press the button even though she really wanted to stab it repeatedly with her finger.

Come on. Come on. Come on!

Marly's mind whirled while she waited for the infernally slow elevator. That was a close one.

Her stomach plummeted as the weight of her actions settled in. Snooping around in your boss's office was never a smart idea for a lot of reasons, but Marly had a more pressing reason than most. She glanced back toward his office, a twinge of guilt pinching her gut. Jasper hadn't been irate when he'd found her in his liquor cabinet. He hadn't yelled and kicked her out or fired her as she might have expected. He'd acted nice. Interested.

She was starting to get the impression that Jasper Kenney wasn't the cold-hearted monster he was reputed to be, and if that was true, it would make her job that much more difficult.

JASPER STARED at the doorway through which Marly had just disappeared. Her vanilla-lemon scent lingered in the air, causing a strange and unwanted longing in his chest. And a tickle in his nose.

"Well, *she* seems interesting." Edward gave a pointed glance at the two drink glasses and then Jasper's wet pants before walking over to the small stocked bar in the office to pour himself a drink.

Jasper knew what his father meant by "interesting." He clearly had the wrong idea. Defensiveness flared.

Leave it to his father to think that Marly had been here for more than just work.

Then again, it was after hours, an odd time for a meeting, especially one Jasper couldn't remember scheduling. Had Veronica really scheduled it? He wouldn't be surprised if she was up to something—she'd been acting very odd ever since Marly had been put on the special project.

"She is a very good employee. I'm happy with her work so far," Jasper said crisply.

"She certainly isn't like most of the young women here, though. She's a bit overweight. Is that the image you want Draconia to project?" Edward studied Jasper so intently that he felt uncomfortable.

Jasper's eyes flicked to the photo of his mother. She'd never liked the way Edward had been so hung up on appearances. Edward had run the company with an iron fist, and he'd never paid attention to anything his mother —or anyone else—said on the matter of appearances. It was, after all, a fashion company, and appearance was important.

But it was Jasper's company now. And maybe the company image needed to change—things certainly weren't going so well the way it was now.

"What image is that, Dad? The stick-thin overly expensive suit and stiletto heel image the rest of the women here portray? I'm more worried about her ability to work than her looks." Jasper barked the words at his father, which was unusual. He rarely raised his voice at Edward. Was he being overly sensitive about

Marly? Why?

"Calm down, Jasper. I was merely pointing something out. You know I tend to be a bit picky when it comes to how the employees here dress and look. Looks are everything in this industry, whether you like it or not. Since you run the largest fashion house in the world, I assume you know something about looks," Edward said coldly, almost in a bored tone. "Let's go eat. I am starving."

Going out for dinner was the last thing Jasper wanted to do, especially with his father, but he reluctantly agreed. He knew Edward Kenney didn't take no for an answer without a fight.

9

T anner Durcotte slammed his fist down on the conference room table. They had been in this meeting arguing for over an hour, and it was late. His design team at Theorim Fashions just wasn't getting it.

"I do not, again, *do not* care what you think of these designs. Get working on them. Modify them a little if you need to, but just *do it*! I am the CEO. No one else. If you don't like what I'm telling you, then you can leave. Understood?" he asked, looking around the room at the sea of stunned faces.

"Tanner, we just want to ensure we have the best fall line for the runway show." Marcy Nichols, the Vice President of Design, did not raise her voice. She had worked for Tanner for ten years and knew him well. The designs he had brought into the meeting weren't anything she or her team wanted to work with. She also knew better than to argue with him at this point, especially given the bright-red color of his angry face.

"Get to work finishing them, then!" Tanner bellowed and stormed out of the conference room. He marched into his office and slammed the door shut. Everyone thought the designs he had presented were hideous. Why was that?

A niggle of doubt manifested in the back of Tanner's mind. According to Marly, Draconia had spent three years working on them. Would they spend that much time on something that wasn't any good? But he was sure his own staff knew what they were talking about, and they'd *hated* them.

Something wasn't right here, and he didn't have time for a screwup. The fall fashion show was only a few weeks away. He grabbed his phone and called Marly.

MARLY DIDN'T bother to look at her phone when she heard it ring. She knew who it was.

Tanner.

She would deal with him later. *After* her mental breakdown over what had just happened upstairs in Jasper's office. She couldn't stop replaying it over and over in her mind.

What would she have told him about the reports if Veronica hadn't interrupted? She could have bluffed her way through something—she knew the information cold —but it had been stupid for her to risk getting caught in his office in the first place. Where was her common sense?

The corners of Marly's lips quirked up when she replayed the look on Veronica's face when she opened the door. Of course she must have thought something was going on with the way Marly was on her knees in front of Jasper's chair.

Thinking back about it made Marly's pulse race. She had to admit she'd felt... something... being so close to Jasper. But that was certainly only one-sided. Jasper had his pick of beautiful women, and most of them weren't klutzes that spilled drinks on him.

She'd heard all the stories of Jasper being a womanizer, and she knew he could have any woman he wanted. The women in the office always commented on his good looks, even the married ones. The fact he was the CEO and so wealthy made him one of the most eligible bachelors in New York.

Pushing Jasper to the back of her mind, she scooped up all the binders she had printed out and assembled for the meeting, giving them one final glance to ensure they were accurate and consistent.

She headed to the conference room and placed one at each seat. Better to get it set up now instead of rushing around tomorrow morning. The conference room wasn't going to be used until the meeting tomorrow, which worked out nicely.

She proceeded to do a dry run of her presentation to make sure she wasn't fumbling around with her laptop in the actual meeting. Even though she knew the information cold, she was worried about the slides and the mechanics of switching to the right slide on her computer. She was famous for hitting the wrong button and would be embarrassed if that happened. As stupid as it sounded, it was the little things that could make your presentation seem unprofessional.

She spent much longer than she had anticipated on her practice run and was glad because she had come across a few mistakes. She corrected them and then updated all the binders carefully.

It was almost nine by the time she finished. She knew she'd better hurry home and try and get some sleep, although sleep seemed unlikely. She had far too much on her mind.

JASPER HIT the P button on the elevator. He couldn't wait to escape to the solitude of his penthouse apartment. Dinner with his father had been exhausting. It always was. Edward had droned on about buying some new properties in upstate New York, while Jasper's mind had been on his flailing sales numbers.

His penthouse was spotless. Not a stray piece of lint on the leather sectional or a spot of dust on the mahogany-and-glass tables. The kitchen didn't have even one errant crumb. The stainless steel appliances glistened, as did the marble floor. Only the low hum of the high-end stainless steel refrigerator could be heard. Inside the fridge, Sarah had placed several prepackaged homemade meals.

Jasper pulled out a container, opened the top, and

sniffed—the scent of garlic and basil hit him. Sarah's meals were always delicious, and he was grateful for all she did for him. Homemade food was much better than the usual frozen foods he had to microwave, or the sandwich meats that always spoiled and had to be thrown away because he never took the time to make a sandwich.

Sure, he'd helped her brother out once when they were desperate, but he didn't expect Sarah to cater to him to make up for it. Good thing Edward had never found out—he'd have read Jasper the riot act. Jasper made a mental note to thank Sarah tomorrow. Maybe give her a raise.

Edward would shit a brick about that. He never gave raises unless he had to. His attitude was that he was doing everyone that worked at Draconia a favor by employing them. Was Edward right? Maybe he would hold off on the raise.

He stripped off his shirt, caught a slight hint of lemon, and sneezed. Marly. The sudden image of her trying to dab at the spilled drink came to mind and made Jasper wonder what it would be like if…

Well, never mind. He didn't want to go there. The drink spill had been an accident. His fault, really, because he'd sneezed and startled her. He was sure there had been nothing suggestive in the way she'd tried to clean it up. It had actually been kind of comical. Innocent and sweet in a way.

Unlike what his father had said, Jasper didn't think Marly was overweight. He thought she was curvy in all the right places, just like a woman should be. He admired her confidence and liked that she stood out amongst the others in the company. He was excited to work with her on this project, and maybe that wasn't all due to the fact that it could help sales. And the sneeze proved it—just as his mother had always said. He'd sneezed when talking about her new designs, and that was a sign to green-light the project in a big way. Marly's presentation might be met with resistance from the executives, but Jasper was already convinced it might be the one thing that could save the company.

10

Marly arrived at the office early, her stomach in knots over the presentation. Why in the world had she ever spoken up in the first place?

She should have just kept her big mouth shut. Now she would have to stand up in front of everyone and give this presentation.

She had spent over an hour picking her clothes for the day and had settled on a black skirt and blazer with a gray blouse underneath. She had pulled her hair back at her neck and wore several silver bracelets and a large chunky necklace as a statement piece. She felt good with what she had on. She felt confident.

The outfit made her look professional, and that was all she was dressing for. To appear professional in front of the executives.

She dropped her purse off at her desk and headed to the conference room, avoiding drinking any coffee. She was jittery enough.

As she opened the door to the conference room, her heart skipped a beat. Shit. It was empty. Where were all the binders she'd carefully placed at each seat?

She ran over to the credenza that was against the wall and opened the doors. Empty.

She stood there in shock. She ran back to her desk. Maybe someone had put everything back on her desk, and she just hadn't noticed it earlier.

There wasn't anything there. She looked under her desk, checked drawers. Nothing.

Her head swam with dizziness. She picked up her phone and called the woman who was in charge of the conference room upkeep, Charlene. Charlene was an older woman, friendly, and her only job was to reserve all the meeting rooms within Draconia, and to ensure the food was taken care of and that they were cleaned up after each meeting.

Marly let the phone ring, drumming her fingers impatiently on the desk. *Answer!*

"Hello?" Relief swept through Marly as Charlene's voice came through the phone.

"Hi, Charlene, this is Marly West. I had placed some binders in conference room 1226 late last night, and they are all gone now. By any chance do you know where they are?" Marly's voice was tight with panic.

"Hi, Miss West. No. No, I don't know anything about that. I had that room cleaned yesterday around noon, and no one has had it reserved again until today," Charlene said cheerfully, unaware that her words caused Marly's chest to tighten so hard she could barely breathe.

"Oh. Umm, okay. Well, if you hear of anyone finding some binders, can you let me know? Thank you so much." Marly hung up and logged onto her computer. She would have to print everything out again. Ten sets!

How would she be able to get that all printed and bound in less than an hour? It had taken her two hours to do it all, and another hour just to do the final review. The printing alone was time consuming, as it was all in color and the color printer was an older one, always getting jammed.

She couldn't believe this was happening to her. She started to print, praying that she would somehow pull off getting everything done in time for the meeting. But she had no choice. She got started running through the tasks as quickly as possible.

"AHEM. EVERYONE IS WAITING FOR YOU." Veronica's snotty voice filtered through the air over to Marly, who was immersed in collating papers.

"Oh my God!" Marly gasped, and her eyes jerked to the clock on the wall. It was nine a.m.

She had been so busy trying to get everything done she had forgotten to set the alarm in her phone for eight forty-five. She wasn't finished! The printer had jammed two times and had then run out of ink. There was no ink in the supply room, and she'd had to run around to two separate floors to find some, which had eaten up a good twenty minutes.

This was a disaster.

She grabbed her blazer, which she had taken off to assemble the papers, and her laptop, leaving all the half-finished handouts behind. She ran after Veronica, pulling on her blazer haphazardly. As she entered the room, she immediately saw Jasper sitting at the head of the table. She felt disheveled and ran a hand over her skirt in an attempt to smooth out the wrinkles that had appeared from sitting so long. This was not how she had wanted to make her entrance. All her careful hours of planning were wasted. She was pissed.

"Now that everyone is here, let's get started. Marly, I would like you to present first." Jasper's face was impassive, but Marly sensed a note of irritation in his voice.

"My apologies for being late, everyone," Marly said, deciding to leave out the part that all the handouts she had spent so much time on had somehow disappeared overnight. She hooked her laptop up to the screen and started with the presentation.

"Sorry to interrupt, Marly, but are there handouts for this? So we can follow along and make notes at our seats versus having to look at the screen the entire time?" Bill White, VP of Sales, asked smugly.

"I'm sorry, Bill. Unfortunately, there are no handouts now, but I will be happy to send you a copy afterwards." Marly forced down the annoyance that was bubbling up inside her. She didn't want that tainting her presentation.

"Not really helpful, but thanks, anyway." Bill smirked.

Marly ignored Bill's rude comment. What a jerk. She had assumed that Bill and Steve Henderson, the VP of

Marketing, would be coming after her in this meeting, since she was pointing out mistakes and weak spots they had each made in their departments.

She had made sure she knew the data inside out, so she wasn't fumbling around for answers. She sailed through the rest of the presentation, going through all the numbers and the marketing campaigns to show the weaknesses and then suggesting areas for improvement.

She ended the presentation with the plus-size line, citing several facts regarding the sudden surge of plus-size models, pointing out how *Vogue* and *Marie Claire* were both using plus-size models in their editions. She had waited for Veronica to laugh when she had started to talk about plus size, or to make a comment asking if Marly wanted that line for herself, but it never came. Veronica was quiet the entire time.

When Marly finished, Jasper stood up.

"Thank you, Marly. That was very informative. You broke it all down for everyone, so I am assuming there aren't any questions. Bill, you're up next." Jasper poured himself another cup of coffee and then sat down again.

The tension drained from Marly's shoulders as she took her seat. Hopefully she hadn't let on how nervous she'd been during the presentation. The truth was she'd been terrified the others, especially Bill and Steve, would eat her alive.

Her gaze flicked to Jasper. She couldn't tell whether he'd been happy with the presentation or not. She was grateful he hadn't opened the room up for questions—

had he done that on purpose to protect her from Bill and Steve?

No, she was overthinking. Jasper would never change his business tactics to protect her. Even though it seemed like he respected her opinion, this was all business to him, and if he thought a Q and A was needed, he would have said so. Make no mistake about it—Jasper Kenney was her boss, not her friend.

As Bill droned on, she couldn't wait for the meeting to be over so she could finish her work for the day and cut out early. She had something much more important than sales numbers and fashion lines to tend to, and she didn't want anyone from Draconia Fashions to know about it.

JASPER WAS HAVING a hard time focusing on that blowhard, Bill Henderson, while he rambled on about pie charts and sales numbers at the front of the conference room.

He had been extremely impressed with Marly's presentation. She had pulled together a lot of information that he hadn't even thought about analyzing. And judging by Bill's lame slides, none of his overly paid executives had thought of analyzing it, either.

Jasper's lips quirked in a smile as he thought about how Marly had deftly handled Henderson's rude comments during her presentation. She had the makings of a true executive.

He already knew he wanted Marly to work on a sample plus-size line. He planned to work closely with her on that purely for the benefit of the business. Nothing personal about it. He didn't get personal with the employees.

He'd set up a meeting with her later, though. He didn't need to get the other executives up in arms about it. And he certainly didn't need Edward to hear about it right now. Something with the word "plus" in it would make Edward lose his shit.

When it was finally over, Jasper asked Veronica to stay back. She trotted back to him, a hopeful look on her face.

"Can you book some time on my calendar with Marly West? We will need about two hours. Not this afternoon. I have my weekly appointment tonight. Book it for later this week."

Veronica's hopeful look turned to suspicion. What was going on with her? Jasper had clued in to the fact that Veronica didn't like Marly. She was probably jealous of Marly's good looks as well as the attention she was getting.

"Of course, Mr. Kenney," Veronica murmured.

"Thanks." He shot the word over his shoulder as he brushed by her on his way out. Veronica was a good assistant, but if her attitude didn't change, he might have to consider getting rid of her. It was affecting her work.

He didn't have time to think about that now. He had a stack of paperwork piled up on his desk that needed his attention before he could leave for the night to attend his weekly appointment.

The appointment was something he wouldn't miss, no matter what came up. He knew the appointment was the object of much speculation amongst the executives, but he would never reveal where he went. It was his personal business, and no one at Draconia needed to know what he was up to.

VERONICA'S HEART hitched as she watched Jasper disappear down the hallway.

"You're welcome," she muttered to herself. Was she imagining it, or was Jasper getting more and more distant?

Of course she wasn't imagining it. It was all because of Marly West. Why did Jasper think Marly was so damn good, anyway?

Maybe she should try to set them up. It would never work out, just like all of Jasper's other girlfriends. And then he'd run off just as he always did when things turned to crap. And when he ran off, the only person he communicated with was her. She'd have him all to herself then. But no, that might backfire. Marly West was different, and she didn't want to take a chance.

Veronica stomped to the elevator, tapping her foot impatiently as she waited for it. Marly had somehow pulled off the presentation, despite Veronica's effort to sabotage it.

Veronica frowned at the memory of the previous night. She'd known Jasper would be working late, and she'd purposely gone home and changed into her most seductive—but still appropriate for work—dress, then returned to the office to try and capture Jasper's attention.

Imagine her surprise to find him holed up in his office with Marly West. She knew they didn't have a meeting, so what had they been doing in there?

Veronica sat behind her desk, eyeing Jasper's closed door. From what she'd seen when she'd walked in, whatever they were doing had very little to do with business. She jerked her middle drawer open. Inside sat a brown package of M&M's. As a rule, Veronica avoided anything high in calories—she had to keep her thin figure, at least until after she got her claws into Jasper. The M&M's were for emergencies. Like now.

She slit the package open with a perfectly manicured cherry-red fingernail and slid out one M&M. Just one wouldn't hurt, would it? She sucked on the confection to make it last. The hard sugar coating gave way to the creamy chocolate inside. She had to admit, eating the M&M did make her feel better.

She tipped another one out into her palm. How many calories were in an M&M? Not many. She could probably work it off in ten minutes on the treadmill. She popped it into her mouth as she thought about the previous night.

After Jasper and Edward had gone to dinner, she'd made her way to Marly's office. Marly had already left for the night. Veronica had noticed the conference room light was on, and when she'd looked in, she'd seen the nice binders Marly had placed there. Marly was trying way too hard—what was she up to?

Veronica had gotten rid of all the binders, chuckling to herself at the time. Now it seemed that the joke was on her, and she didn't like that one bit. She had pictured Marly fumbling around, stuttering, unable to answer questions and bursting into tears. Instead, Marly had been organized and calm, fielding the comments with ease.

The M&M package crinkled as Veronica clenched her fist in frustration. She poured three out into her palm and shoved them in her mouth. Something would have to be done about Miss West. The picture she had of Marly and Tanner Durcotte eating together would come in handy for that.

She could show those to Jasper right now, but what did they prove? Nothing. She needed to know *why* they were together.

Marly was up to something, and Veronica needed to figure out what it was before she showed Jasper the pictures. That way, Marly wouldn't be able to come up with any excuses, and Jasper would see her for the conniving bitch she was. As an added bonus, he would see Veronica as the one who saved him. Win-win!

Veronica looked down at the empty M&M pack in her hand. Had she eaten them all? Damn that Marly West! She had to speed up her plan to get rid of her before she ruined everything, including her size-zero figure.

She shoved the empty M&M wrapper inside her Styrofoam Starbucks cup and tossed it in the trash. She didn't want anyone at work to see that she'd eaten a whole pack of M&M's. Then she spun around to face the computer. She had a lot of work to do, not the least of which was speeding up her plan to show Jasper just how wrong he was about Marly West.

11

The glass-paneled Draconia building loomed over Marly as she walked past it on her way to the hospital. It was four p.m., nearly quitting time, but she still felt guilty leaving early. It wasn't as if anyone noticed, though, and besides, she had worked so many hours over the past week she'd put in more than her share of time.

She had to admit she was enjoying the work—especially the special presentation she'd done that morning. A feeling of regret washed over her. If things were different, she wouldn't mind staying there, maybe even making a career out of it. But that wasn't going to happen, not after she stole the designs.

Marly sprinted up the steps to the hospital, wondering if she should cut down her hours. She needed to spend as much time at the hospital as possible—her mother was getting worse.

The hospital corridors were bustling with nurses. A few patients lay outside their rooms on gurneys, waiting to be transferred back to their beds. Probably returning from a scan or tests done deep in the bowels of the hospital. Those things always seemed to take forever, and Marly was painfully aware that getting the patient back in bed could take a bit of maneuvering.

Her shoes clacked on the shiny green-and-white industrial tile as she weaved her way through the halls. The antiseptic smell of bleach and rubbing alcohol stung her nose. The constant beep beep beeping of machines ticked like a metronome in her ear.

Her stomach clenched with the familiar feeling of doom as she entered the cancer wing. What condition would she find her mother in today?

Marly turned into the room, her eyes falling on the impossibly tiny figure that lay under the blankets in the far bed. The room was a double, but no other patient had been placed in there, so Marly's mom had it all to herself. Marly liked that.

She crept closer to the bed. Her mother was resting peacefully, and Marly felt grateful that she could get some respite from the pain and anxiety of her cancer diagnosis. She hoped her mother was dreaming about better days. Days spent in the sunshine, healthy and full of joy.

Marly stood silently beside the bed. Despair squeezed her heart as she looked at the dozens of purple bruises that surrounded the IV line that fed through the parchment-like skin into her mother's frail hand, delivering fluids and various medicines.

Her mother's skin was pale, her once full pink lips now thin and dry with almost a blue tinge to them. Marly kissed her on the forehead gently so as not to wake her and then sat down.

The blue vinyl hospital chair was surprisingly comfortable, and Marly sank back into it, her eyes drifting to the window. Outside, horns honked and people made their way down the sidewalks in a bustle of activity. The world still went on for everyone else, even though Marly's world was crashing, dying with the woman who lay in the bed beside her.

Marly rested her head against the back of the chair. She'd been burning the candle at both ends with trying to spend so much time here and working at Draconia. She was mentally and physically exhausted. She knew she had to get the real designs to Tanner soon, but once she did, that would be the end of her job at Draconia.

As her eyes fluttered shut, Marly wondered if there was a way to satisfy Tanner and keep her job.

MARLY'S EYES FLEW OPEN. Had she fallen asleep? It was dark outside now. She looked at her mother, who was still asleep. A nurse was checking her IV.

"How is she?" Marly whispered as she stood up and stretched.

"Oh, hi. I hope I didn't wake you. She's okay. I gave

her some morphine. The doctor increased her dosage earlier. She will be pretty much out of it until ... I mean, for now." The nurse's tone was sympathetic.

Marly knew the nurse had started to say that her mother would be out of it until she died. The doctor had said that without the operation, she was unlikely to last more than a few weeks. Even with it, it was a long shot.

Marly felt a pang of sympathy for the doctor. He'd apologized to her over and over about insurance not covering the operation because they considered it experimental. Marly had told him she would get the money. She needed to make a plan *now* to get the drawings for Tanner.

A feeling of desperation shot through her. She couldn't bear to see her mother like this. Tears pricked the backs of her eyes, and she screwed them shut. She wished she hadn't started to like the job at Draconia so much. The swell of pride she felt that the CEO had singled her out to make suggestions was tainted with bitter regret. She mentally pushed the gnawing guilt at having to steal the company designs away. She knew it could cause Draconia to go out of business, but what choice did she have?

Her mother was dying, and the whole reason she had taken the job at Draconia was to get the drawings for Tanner so she could get the money needed for the operation to save her mom.

She walked over to her mother, whispered, "Mom, I love you," in her ear, and kissed her on the forehead. Her mother didn't move. She was deep in a morphine-induced sleep.

Marly left the room, walking slowly down the hall in a daze, deep in thought. As she approached the nurses' station, a familiar voice wafting out of the family room struck a chord deep inside her.

Her brows dipped together. She knew that voice. Not from the hospital, but she couldn't quite figure out from where.

She stood to the left of the door and peeked into the room. There were about a dozen kids inside, some in wheelchairs, some sitting on the floor on large beanbags, most with IVs attached to their frail arms. In front of them, facing away from her, was a man reading a book to them.

Marly's heart stopped. The man was Jasper Kenney.

She couldn't believe it. It made no sense. Why would Jasper Kenney, of all people, be reading to a bunch of sick kids? He seemed kind of uptight and so... well... important and disconnected.

Marly tiptoed back to the nurses' station. "Excuse me. What's going on in there?" Marly pointed toward the room.

"We have story time for the kids a few times a week. This particular one is kind of late every week, but it's meant for the kids who have labs and testing done late in the day on Tuesdays. We found it helps them relax and calms them so they can sleep," the nurse replied, busy looking at charts.

"That's really great. Do the people who read to them

work here?" Marly asked even though she already knew the answer.

"Some do, but not the one run on Tuesdays. He is a volunteer. Really nice guy. The kids love him. He's pretty easy on the eyes, too! He's a donor here, too. In fact, I'm pretty sure the family room exists because of his generosity." The nurse leaned in and whispered, "We call him our guardian angel."

The nurse slipped back behind the desk to answer the phone, and Marly made a beeline for the stairs, rushing past the room where Jasper sat.

She had sat in that family room many times before. It was an area for the cancer patients and their families, and it was wonderful. It had several computers in it, a huge library, tons of toys, a massive television, and a kitchen with a coffee bar. It made the difficult situation everyone on that floor faced a bit easier.

Had Jasper paid for all that? Why? She didn't think the executives at Draconia were the philanthropic type. In fact, she was sure Bill, Steve, and Edward would never donate their time to read to critically ill children. She wouldn't have thought Jasper would, either, but here he was.

Marly realized she actually didn't know very much about him. Apparently, he *was* the type to read to ill children. And he was a fair boss and shrewd businessman. Not the monster she'd read about.

Marly felt an unwanted tug at her heart. Jasper Kenney was turning out to be *nothing* like she'd thought he'd be. He was actually likable—very likable. And if the butterflies in her stomach and hitch in her chest every time he was near her were any indication, she could easily fall for him.

And that would be a huge mistake because it would make screwing him over that much more difficult.

JASPER CLOSED the book just as he caught a glimpse of fluttering dark curls out of the corner of his eye. His mind wandered to Marly. Why did he keep thinking about her? She kept creeping into his thoughts at inopportune moments, and it was unsettling. Jasper hadn't met a woman that crept into his thoughts like that in a long time.

For a split second, he let himself entertain the thought that he could have a relationship with Marly. There were so many reasons that would never happen. Besides, he barely knew the girl.

Edward would be outraged, not only because she was an employee, but because Edward thought Marly was overweight. A jolt of rebellion flashed through Jasper. He was tired of doing what Edward would think was the right thing. Maybe it was time he stood up to the old man, once and for all.

Jasper said goodbye to the kids and the nurses and headed out into the hallway, his chest tightening when he caught a whiff of vanilla and lemon. Marly.

Was she here?

He whirled around and saw nothing but an empty

hallway. Great, now his mind was playing tricks on him. He turned back around, walking faster, stifling a sneeze. He couldn't wait to get home and bury himself in work that would stop these insistent thoughts about Marly West from messing with his brain.

12

"Hey, stranger. What's new?" Marly turned around, waiting for Sarah to wade through the after-lunch rush and catch up to her in the vast Draconia lobby.

"Hi! Same old, same old here," Marly said.

"I heard through the grapevine you did well on your presentation for Jasper." Sarah grinned as they stepped onto the elevator.

"You did? From who?" Marly was surprised. She knew it couldn't have come from Veronica.

"I overheard Jasper talking on the phone yesterday about it," Sarah said, rummaging around in her bag for something. "Something about making you in charge of a new line or something? You go, girl!"

"New line? No, I think you misunderstood. I suggested a new line. That's cool he's thinking about it, but I'm sure he'd have Bill or Steve head that up."

The elevator stopped on Marly's floor, and Sarah

shoved a Tupperware container at her as Marly exited the elevator.

"Here. Try this, please. I'll call you later on!" Sarah yelled as the elevator doors shut.

A thrill of excitement buzzed through Marly. Jasper had liked her presentation! But the excitement was squashed just as soon as it came. With her mother as sick as she was, Marly couldn't feel excited about much, and anyway, it didn't matter if Jasper liked her presentation. She had no future at Draconia.

She turned on her computer, and a meeting reminder flashed on her monitor. Shit! She had a meeting with Jasper in ten minutes.

When did that get booked? She hadn't seen anything about it all morning. It must have been Veronica, screwing with her probably and turning off the option for the attendee to confirm on purpose. She was such a bitch!

Marly grabbed her purse and raced to the bathroom. Her hair looked like an unruly mess, one of the hazards of walking to work. She smoothed it down and put a dab of lip gloss on over her full lips. She brushed on a bit of bronzer. As if Jasper cared about her looks.

Back at her desk, she called upstairs to Sarah.

"Hey, I guess I have a meeting with your boss in a few minutes. I'm gonna come up now. Can you let me in? I don't want to deal with you know who," Marly said. Better not to reveal that she knew the access code.

"Of course I can. See you in a few minutes," Sarah replied.

Marly got off the elevator and pulled Sarah aside. "Thanks. I'm pissed I had a whopping ten minutes notice for the meeting. Any idea what it's about?"

"I looked it up, but there were no details about it. Sorry. I mean, usually we wait for people to accept the meeting request, you know? Veronica's just an ass at times about this stuff. It's happened before, so don't feel bad," Sarah explained.

Marly was relieved to hear it had happened before. She was starting to feel that Veronica St. James had it in for her, and she had no idea why.

"That makes me feel better. Thanks, Sarah. I appreciate it." She really meant it. Sarah was a good person to know at Draconia.

Sarah tapped on Jasper's door, and Marly was flooded with a sudden rush of nervousness. The memory of seeing him reading to the children at the hospital surfaced, and she relaxed a little, knowing he had a softer side. Should she mention it? No, she was sure he didn't want anyone from work to know, and she would have to explain why she was there. She didn't want Jasper or anyone else feeling sorry for her.

"Hi, Marly. Come on in," Jasper said in a professional, welcoming tone. Marly eyed the coffee table. Hopefully, this meeting wasn't about the drink incident. Maybe now that she'd made her presentation, Jasper had no need for a klutzy drink-spilling fatty on his sales team, and he was calling her here to fire her.

Marly thanked Sarah as she passed by her, and headed toward one of the chairs across from Jasper's desk. She felt stupid for not knowing what he wanted to meet about and decided she needed to let him know she wasn't sure why she was there, in case he thought she was unprepared.

"Hi, Jasper. I came up as soon as I saw the meeting request this morning, and there wasn't an agenda, so I'm not sure if you needed me to bring anything with me," she ventured.

"I just wanted to talk about the plus-size line you spoke about yesterday. I'm a little surprised Veronica didn't attach the agenda for you." Jasper was typing on his keyboard and didn't look up at Marly. "I can print your presentation from here anyway."

"Sorry about that. I actually had a binder of it for you, but it disappeared prior to the meeting yesterday." Marly hoped she didn't sound whiny. So there *had* been an agenda. She was almost certain now that Veronica was purposely trying to make her look like an idiot, and she wasn't going to let that happen. *Screw you, Veronica. Two can play at this game.*

"Looking over the plus-size line proposal, I was intrigued. The revenue you projected is extremely high. I assume you did your research with whoever would be our main competitor? Not Theorim, since they don't have a plus line. Yet," Jasper said, emphasizing the word "yet." Marly squirmed in her chair at the mention of Theorim. It reminded her that she needed to get Tanner his damn drawings ASAP.

"I did all the research. VasDenso Designs would be our main competitor. They don't have the same following as we do, so I do think this could be something we could quickly surpass them in sales-wise."

"Excellent. VasDenso had a record quarter recently." Jasper plucked a spreadsheet off the printer behind him and studied it.

"Yes, they did. The plus line increased their sales by twenty-eight percent." Marly could recite the numbers in her sleep—the information was ingrained in her head. "There's an entire movement toward larger sizes for women. Bluntly, I don't think a double-digit size is "plus," but most designers do. The reality is some women who are in great shape wear larger sizes. So why discriminate against them, and have lines stop at size eight?"

Marly didn't want to come off as an angry curvy girl. The fact she had lost so much weight and still had to buy many clothes in the Plus or Misses sections pissed her off. She wasn't fat. It was time top designers started realizing women were embracing healthy lifestyles versus starving themselves to fit into tiny sizes.

"I like the fire in your eyes when you talk about this. I'm putting *you* in charge of this new line. It's due in a few weeks, so you have your work cut out for you." Jasper sat back in his chair, staring intently across the desk at Marly.

"What? Me? No. I… I mean, thank you, Jasper, but that is a really big r-responsibility, and I have only been here a few m-months," Marly stammered.

Dammit! It would be her dream come true to be in charge of a whole clothing line, but she couldn't do it. She needed to focus on getting those fall designs for

Tanner. She could not be distracted with a huge responsibility that would be all for nothing once her treachery was discovered.

"I wouldn't give you the task if I didn't think you could do it. Don't you think you can handle it?"

Across the table, Jasper's blue eyes glimmered with the challenge. Instead of the cold, sharklike stare she'd seen at the first meeting, she saw something deeper under the surface. He was trusting her with something that, if not done correctly, could cause his company to potentially go out of business.

The sad truth was she *could* handle the job. She was ready for this responsibility, but she couldn't accept. Unless...

An idea sparked in Marly's brain. She knew this new responsibility would give her higher access to the company design portfolio and tools. Maybe this new job could be the way to save her mother and have her dream, too.

She looked Jasper directly in the eye. "I can do it."

Marly's heart stuttered as Jasper's face broke out into a dimpled grin. Damn, the guy was cute. And her boss. And one of the most eligible bachelors in New York with plenty of more interesting women than Marly to hang around with.

"Good. I noticed your laptop at the meeting. It's an older one. I've arranged for a new one for you, and you have access to whatever you need as well—all the past designs, the new fall line, and the other designers. You should get it sometime today. We will have to work closely on this because of the timeline and critical nature. You're okay with that, right?"

"Absolutely."

"Good. I think this project is going to be very good for the company." Jasper returned his attention to his computer.

Marly pushed herself up from the chair. "Well, if that's all, then I guess I'll go back to my desk and get started."

"Yes. Thank you." He never even looked up from the computer, proving Marly's theory that he had no romantic intentions toward her whatsoever.

She headed to Sarah's desk.

"How'd it go?" Sarah asked.

"Good. Great, actually." Marly had decided it was best not to talk too much about what the meeting had been about. She wasn't sure Jasper wanted people to know about it, although she highly doubted it was a secret.

"When you're done chitchatting, I have some errands you need to run for Mr. Kenney." An obnoxiously loud voice interrupted them. Veronica.

Marly rolled her eyes, making Sarah giggle.

"Yes, ma'am!" Sarah semi-yelled back at Veronica, who was now walking away in a huff.

"She's so uptight. I think I've had maybe two decent conversations with her!" Sarah said to Marly as they both headed down the hall.

"Well, that's two more than I've had." Marly stopped at the elevator. "I'll talk to you later."

Sarah split off toward Veronica's desk, and Marly got on the elevator. Once she was inside, the reality of what she was just put in charge of started to settle in, and a seed of doubt gnawed at her stomach. Could she really pull it off?

Her cell phone blared an ominous Darth Vader ringtone just as she sat at her desk. Tanner. She'd programmed the tone specifically for him because it was always doom and gloom whenever he got on the phone.

"When will you have the rest of the drawings?" Tanner demanded.

"Gee. No hello or how are you? Tanner, I need some time. I mean, I gave you four already. They are still working on them here as it is," she lied.

"Marly, you know the deal. And I assume you need the money sooner rather than later. Or is your mother on the rebound now?" Tanner asked.

Marly cheeks burned. Tanner knew her mother's cancer was not "on the rebound." She needed the procedure and subsequent chemo after for a remission to even be possible.

"Don't you think I would have given you them all if I could have by now, Tanner? I'm working on getting them as soon as I can for you. They aren't exactly something I have access to. I'll talk to you later." Marly hung up.

To hell with Tanner Durcotte. Her mother was dying, and Tanner was the only person who could help her. Some family friend he was. He'd known they were broke and that they needed money for her mother's procedure when he'd come to her with the plan for her to get a position at Draconia and steal the designs. Once she turned them over, he would pay for everything.

Getting the job had been no problem—she was more than qualified—but getting her hands on the designs turned out to be a lot harder than she'd anticipated. Who knew they kept them so closely guarded?

Tanner had never mentioned a deadline, but now he was putting the screws to her. But even if he wasn't turning up the heat, she needed to get them to him right away—her mother was slipping away fast, and soon she would be too far gone for the procedure to help.

Marly tapped the keys to wake up her computer. She would have to work fast if she wanted to put her new plan into action.

JASPER WAS SURPRISINGLY EXCITED that Marly had accepted the position. Sure, the new plus-size line would be a boon for the company, but his excitement went beyond that. Marly's excitement and passion for the new project was contagious, and he hadn't felt that passion for a project in a long time—not since his mother had been alive and he'd been a junior executive learning the ropes. And he hadn't sneezed once when looking over the designs. Another sign—Jasper liked to think it was from his mom—that he was doing the right thing. She'd always teased that his sneezing indicated an opportunity right under his nose that he shouldn't let pass by, and once he accepted that opportunity, the sneezing stopped.

Jasper knew that passion fueled greatness. Neither Bill nor Steve had ever shown that type of enthusiasm.

Jasper looked over the financial report he had just been sent from the CFO and leaned back in his chair. Gazing out his office window, he watched a bird fly around the patio, darting from one piece of furniture to another.

He rubbed his fingers on his chin, something he did when he was worried. The company was not doing well, and he needed something drastic to pull them out. He'd entrusted Marly with a lot of responsibility, but somehow he knew he had made the right decision.

Edward would be pissed about the plus-size project, but for once, he wasn't afraid of what his father thought. Draconia was his company now, and he'd do whatever it took to make sure they succeeded.

13

Marly slammed her hands on her desk in frustration. She wasn't able to log on to her computer because IT had already set up her new one, which was nowhere to be found. It was already four in the afternoon, and she needed that computer today! She picked up her phone and dialed Sarah's extension.

"Hey, do you know anything about a new laptop Jasper had IT get me?" She didn't want to deal with the IT department directly. They took forever, and she knew Sarah would have an answer.

"Uh-oh. Shit," Sarah said.

"What? What's uh-oh?" Marly asked.

"Well, remember when Veronica told me I had to do errands earlier? One of them was dropping a laptop off at Jasper's. It was a new Mac," Sarah said.

"How do you know it was mine? I assumed IT would have just brought it to me and hooked it up."

"They get stupid when Jasper calls them directly. All

nervous and stuff. They probably dropped it off up here because they wanted him to know they had done it, and then Veronica didn't get the message it was for you and assumed it was for Jasper's home," Sarah said, slowing down at the end. "Or did she?"

"Did she what? Sarah, between you and me, I feel like she doesn't like me and is trying to screw me over or something," Marly confided.

"It wouldn't surprise me if she was. But this would look bad on her, not you. Although she will probably throw the IT guys under the bus and say they didn't tell her it was yours."

"So now what do I do? I wanted to work from home tonight, and my other laptop isn't able to sign on to any of the servers now because they must have killed the access from it when they enabled access on the new one." Marly was irritated. When Jasper had said she'd get access to all the designs, it was like a ray of hope. She needed to bust ass if she was going to put her plan into action, and she needed to do it *tonight*. She couldn't believe that such an established company had so many screwups. Or maybe it was just her bad luck.

"Well, let me see, and I will call you back in a few minutes, okay?"

"Okay." Marly chewed her bottom lip, tapping her fingers on her desk as she waited for Sarah's call back. There wasn't much else she *could* do.

The phone rang, causing her to jump. It was Sarah.

"Okay, I was right, and it is at Jasper's. He's furious.

Not at you, but at Veronica and the IT peeps. But he said you can come get it now."

Marly's eyes widened. "Huh? Get it where?"

"Jasper's. You know he lives in the building right next door, right? In the penthouse."

Marly took a deep breath. At his *house*? She couldn't go there! But she needed that laptop *now*. And besides, she was a professional with a job to do. What was the big deal about going to the boss's house? He'd probably just shove the laptop out the door at her. Or have his butler do it.

"I didn't know that, but I guess it makes sense. You mean the one directly next to us on the left? So do I just go there and head to the penthouse? Does he know I'm coming?" She hoped she didn't sound childlike or insecure, even though she was feeling both.

Sarah laughed. "Why do you sound scared? It's just Jasper. Yes, the one on the left. Yeah, I will tell him you are on your way. No big deal."

Sarah hung up, and Marly stared at the phone. Was she really going to have to go to Jasper's *penthouse*? She had no choice. She *had* to go get the laptop. But even while part of her didn't want to go, a little jolt of excitement ran through another part of her. Especially when she thought about how his blue eyes weren't always cold and the kind way he'd read to those children at the hospital.

Jasper Kenney wasn't always a corporate shark. And she couldn't help but feel as if they had some kind of connection. It turned her insides to mush.

She grabbed her purse and headed on her way, not even stopping in the ladies' room to check herself out. What did it matter how she looked? She couldn't indulge in any schoolgirl fantasies about Jasper. Her mother's life depended on it.

14

The lobby at 2010 Park Place made Marly feel like a midget. It was gargantuan, with open hallways that looked down at the marble-lined walls and floors from twenty stories up. Glass elevators stopped at different levels, the people getting in and out in various states of attire.

It was more like the lobby of an upscale hotel than an apartment building, which was exactly what Marly had always thought it was. There was even a doorman to let her in and a concierge desk. She looked uncertainly at the front desk. Should she announce that she was here to visit Jasper?

"Excuse me, miss, can I help you?" a friendly voice asked her from behind.

Marly turned to find an older gentleman in a suit standing there.

"Oh, hello. No, I am just visiting someone. Jasper Kenney," Marly replied.

"Oh! Of course. You must be Marly. Mr. Kenney is expecting you. I'm Robert. Let me show you to Mr. Kenney's apartment."

He walked Marly over past the bank of glass elevators, around a corner to another single elevator. Above it read Penthouse Access Only. He inserted a key card, and the door opened up.

He gestured for her to step in and followed her into the mahogany-paneled elevator, pressing the P button.

"This is a gorgeous building," Marly said.

"Yes, it is. Thank you. It was renovated about ten years ago. It used to be offices. Now it's all apartments—technically townhomes. *Luxury* townhomes," Robert said.

"Have you worked here long?" Marly asked even though his sense of pride in the building told her that he had.

"Oh, yes. I've worked for the Kenney family for almost thirty years now. I started here in this building and never left," Robert said with a smile.

"Is this building owned by the Kenneys? I didn't realize that."

"Yes, ma'am. Well, technically, they sold the building to individuals who purchased the townhouses. But they own a portion of it as well as maintain it and still run it—the concierge services and the like. It's like a small city inside here," Robert explained as the elevator came to a stop. He again inserted his card, and the doors opened up.

Robert stepped out, holding the elevator door for Marly. They were in a hallway, which had two large plush leather chairs on either side of a double set of doors. Robert rang a buzzer, and after several seconds, Jasper appeared.

He was wearing a blue T-shirt that hugged his muscular chest, showed off his biceps, and deepened his sky-blue eyes. His hair was slightly messy, as if he'd been running his hands through it. The entire look was a deep departure from his usual stuffy-CEO look, and when he cracked that dimpled smile, Marly's heart flipped over.

Stop it—you're just here to get a laptop.

"Miss West is here, sir. Can I get you anything?" Robert asked Jasper.

"Thank you, Robert. No. No, we will be fine. Go enjoy the Yankees game." Jasper grinned at Robert and winked. Robert smiled, shook Marly's hand, and headed back onto the elevator.

Jasper's place was exactly how Marly had imagined it would be. Huge. Floor-to-ceiling windows. Very contemporary furniture—white leather, mostly. Black tiled floors, probably granite. There was an outdoor patio that looked as if it ran the entire length of the apartment. It also had an outdoor fireplace, the kind that had the rocks in it and ran with the flick of a switch. Marly found herself gaping at the extravagance.

"What?" Jasper asked her as he walked toward the patio.

"Hmm? Oh, nothing." Jesus, she sounded like a bimbo.

"You think my place is ridiculous, don't you? Pretentious?" Jasper looked at her intently as if he really cared what she thought. Did he? With his hands shoved in his pockets, he reminded her of a little boy looking for her approval.

Marly's heartbeat picked up speed at the notion that he might care what she thought. No, that was crazy. He'd probably entertained gorgeous supermodels in this same penthouse. Why would he care what she thought?

"No! Not at all. This is gorgeous. I just...well, it suits you well." Marly didn't know what to say. She didn't want to come off as rude. And she wasn't trying to be. It was an amazing place. It just was a little over the top for her tastes.

"Now maybe you see why I said me having a car was a bit ridiculous. It's a five-minute walk to work."

Marly laughed. "Oh, yeah. Well, I guess you still need to get around, and I'm sure get away at times, too." Marly wondered where her laptop was. She didn't spot it anywhere, and the place was so clean it would have stood out.

"When Sarah called me to say you would be by to pick up your laptop, she also reminded me she had stuffed my fridge with some of her latest food creations. If you aren't in a rush, I thought we could perhaps have a working dinner? I know it's last minute, but I'm eager to start on the fall line for your plus size and thought we could go over a few things now, as the next few weeks I will be traveling and out of the office a lot."

Jasper's demeanor was nonchalant, which put Marly at ease. This really was just going to be all business, which suited her just fine, despite the jab in her heart when he said he would be traveling and out of the office a lot. What was up with that?

She was in a hurry to get going so she could get the designs for Tanner but didn't want to seem suspicious to Jasper. What budding designer would turn down a working dinner with the CEO? No one. One more hour wouldn't hurt, she supposed.

"Sounds good to me, as long as you're okay with me throwing ideas out versus having them down for you to look at. I didn't have access to my files most of the day because of this laptop snafu." Marly was surprised at herself for being so cool and collected. She really wanted to get that laptop home, alone, but didn't want to be rude. Plus, she had to admit part of her couldn't resist Jasper's dinner invitation.

"Sorry about that. There was some mix-up with IT and Veronica. Let's eat outside." Jasper motioned toward the patio.

"Okay. How about you get my laptop so I can write as we discuss ideas, and I'll grab the food."

"Deal. The kitchen is over there. Feel free to snoop around," Jasper said as he headed down a hallway, Marly assumed to get her laptop.

The townhouse was open concept, so she couldn't really miss the gourmet kitchen, which opened up into the living room. The two were separated by a granite-topped breakfast bar. The dark-mahogany cabinets complemented sparkling stainless steel appliances.

Opening the fridge, she saw the containers Sarah had left him. They were all labeled with delicious-sounding entrees. She wasn't sure what Jasper wanted and didn't want to yell across the townhouse to ask, so she decided to heat up a few dishes and they could pick at them. Shrimp Alfredo, steak in garlic sauce, green beans with slivered almonds, homemade rosemary bread.

The smells made her mouth water. She rummaged in the cabinets for platters and plates, placing the two main dishes on a large platter then cutting the steak into pieces. She put the green beans in a bowl and placed the bread on another platter, adding some butter to it. She grabbed the main platter and bread and headed outside, where Jasper was already sitting. He stood up to open the door for her.

"Wow. That smells great," he said.

"Here, you take these, and I'll grab the rest." Marly handed him the platters then headed back inside for the green beans, plates, and silverware.

She placed everything on the glass patio table and sat down in the cushioned bamboo chair.

"Drinks. We need drinks. Is white wine okay? Water? Soda?" Jasper asked.

Marly thought back to the last time they had had a drink together. She hoped she wasn't going to spill something on him again.

"White wine would be fine, and a glass of water also, if you don't mind."

Jasper went inside to get the drinks, giving Marly a chance to appreciate her surroundings. It was a beautiful summer night in New York, a gentle breeze blowing the air enough to make it almost time to wear a light sweater. She could hear the muffled traffic down below, but it was far enough away so as to create a background noise, which was more pleasant than the annoyance it would be on the street level.

The patio was about thirty feet wide and fifty feet long, a solid concrete slab. It had oversized couches that were shaped in an "L" configuration, with a large coffee table in front made out of slate. There was a separate seating area around the fireplace. The entire patio was full of various flowers in floor vases and lush green bushes in giant pots, giving it the feeling that you were in a backyard instead of the top of a twenty-story building.

Jasper walked back out onto the patio, a bottle of wine and two glasses in one hand and water in the other. He set them down on the table and poured Marly some wine.

"Before we start, I have to mention something." Jasper's tone turned serious.

Marly's stomach clenched. Did he know what she was up to with Tanner?

"This food that Sarah has been making, do you know anything about it? I mean, it's delicious. I didn't know she was such a good cook until recently." Jasper put a heaping serving of the shrimp Alfredo on his plate.

Marly breathed a sigh of relief.

"She's going to culinary arts school. You didn't know? So she's been making up all kinds of variations of food lately for her classes. I agree with you that they are delicious," Marly explained to him, taking a small portion of the steak. She would have loved a giant slab of it but was determined to stay on her diet. Fifty pounds down, and twenty more to go.

"Hmm. Not sure I knew that. I know I should. She's had a few jobs, and it's hard to keep up. Great girl, though," Jasper said as he worked his way through his food. He had a healthy appetite and apparently wasn't "all knowing" since he didn't realize Sarah was going to culinary school. For some reason, that put Marly at ease. Jasper was human, just like everyone else.

She liked this side of him. He was more relaxed, casual. More like a friend than the boss at the office. *Better not get too comfortable,* her inner voice warned.

They finished eating, and Jasper suggested they move to the area by the fireplace as he handed Marly her laptop.

"Wow. Thanks. This is really more than I needed." Marly couldn't hide her excitement. It was a top-of-the-line Mac. Better than what anyone else in the office had.

"You don't have to thank me. To be honest, I was embarrassed when I saw your laptop at the meeting, and it made me realize our IT department hasn't exactly been keeping up with technology. I know it costs money, but it's worth the expense." Jasper settled into a chair.

"Well, this will be a huge help to me with the designs. And since we are on such a short timeline, I need all the help I can get." Marly sat down across from the fireplace and logged on to the laptop.

"Marly, don't take this the wrong way, but the way you dress is exactly why I know you will make this new line a success. You clearly know how to accentuate the positive," Jasper said.

Marly looked up from her screen, unsure of how to respond. Was he flirting? Or was this normal talk, since they were in the fashion industry? It must be normal talk. But what if it wasn't?

"Thanks. I try," she mumbled, wanting to smack herself as soon as she said it. She sounded so stupid and immature.

She grabbed her wine glass and knocked back the contents. Jasper poured her more.

"So let's brainstorm this new line." Jasper moved to the chair next to Marly, causing her heartbeat to kick up a notch. This was ridiculous. She couldn't get all hot and bothered when Jasper was around, or she'd never be able to work with the man.

For the next hour, Marly focused on telling Jasper about her vision for the new plus-size line. He seemed genuinely interested. He even kicked in some ideas of his own, and they were great ideas, too. Apparently, he wasn't just a CEO—he had an artistic eye for design too. Marly incorporated the ideas on the fly and then added some of her own tweaks on top. It was fun, like designing with a friend, and for a while she forgot that Jasper was the CEO and she was the lowly clerk... and about her extracurricular activities with Tanner.

Jasper seemed just as excited, too, and that made *her* even more excited. Before she knew it, the sun had gone down, and a chill crept into the air. Clouds had rolled in. Marly excused herself so she could grab her blazer.

"No need for your blazer. That's an easy fix," Jasper said, standing up and flicking a switch on the fireplace.

"Thanks. This is all so beautiful. You must spend a lot of time out here."

"I wish. Actually, this is the first time I have been out here in months. I just never take the time to enjoy it, especially lately with sales dwindling." Jasper poured them both more wine. "I don't usually worry too much about the other fashion houses, but I'm starting to. Mostly Theorim. Tanner has something up his sleeve. I can sense it."

Marly's heart skidded. Maybe Jasper *was* on to her. Maybe he'd called her here on the pretext of going over the new line in order to see what she knew and then confront her. But why would he go to this trouble? Feeding her dinner? Giving her wine? No, he had no idea of her treachery.

"Is Tanner the CEO?" she asked innocently.

"Yes. They're our main competitor... well, you probably know that, right?" Jasper asked, sounding concerned.

"Oh, I know, I just don't really pay attention to the people other than the designers. I did all that research on them, remember? The sales figures. Anyway, we will have an awesome fall line, so don't worry." Marly kept her voice light despite the fact that her heart was pounding and she felt like an asshole pretending not to know who Tanner Durcotte was.

Jasper trusted her, and she was going to screw him over. She had no choice, but she knew it would end her job at Draconia. And her friendship with Jasper... if that was what it was. Too bad she actually loved what she was doing, and felt she was kicking ass doing it. She would be blacklisted from the industry when word got around about what she'd done.

"You look as worried as I am," Jasper said to her, laughing. "You have put my mind at ease, though, Marly. I trust you with this new line."

Hearing that made Marly feel worse, not better. A pang of guilt pierced her heart.

"Thanks. I should get going now. I have some work to do in my office before I head home." Marly was starting to feel a little buzz from the wine, and she didn't want it to affect her decisions.

Working out here on the patio with the fire was too close for comfort. Marly desperately wanted to get away before she lost her resolve about giving Tanner the designs. She couldn't let her mother down.

"I'll help you clean up." Marly shot up from her chair and started gathering the glasses and plates from the table.

"No. Let me do that." Jasper tugged at the plates in her hand.

"No, really, I'll bring them in." Marly pulled them back.

"You're my guest..." Jasper reached out and tugged at the plates again. This was silly, but Marly wasn't used to being waited on. Maybe it was time to let someone else clean up.

Their eyes met.

"Fine," they both said at the same time and let go of the plates, which smashed on the floor at their feet.

Marly's hand flew to her mouth. "I'm so sorry!"

She bent down to try to pick up the mess, but she slid on some Alfredo sauce. Her feet went out from under her, and her arms cartwheeled in the air as she fell backwards. Her butt hit the hard concrete patio floor two seconds before her head.

She must have blacked out, because the next thing she knew, Jasper's face was hovering over hers, a concerned expression in his eyes.

"Marly, are you okay?"

She took a mental inventory of her body. Her butt hurt, and it felt wet. She had a slight headache starting, but otherwise, the only thing she was suffering from was acute embarrassment.

"I'm fine." She struggled up onto her elbows.

Jasper placed his hand on her shoulder. "Maybe you shouldn't get up. I can call an ambulance."

An ambulance? That was the last thing she wanted. Maybe he was worried about a lawsuit and wanted to make sure he was covered, but she had work to do. She couldn't spend half the night in the emergency room.

"I'm fine. Really. I'm sorry about the mess."

"Don't worry about it. It's nothing. Are you sure you're okay?"

Marly squinted at Jasper. He seemed genuinely concerned. "I'm sure."

"You have sauce in your hair." He reached out and

flicked at her hair then more gently tucked a strand behind her ear.

Maybe it was the shared passion for the project. Or maybe it was the concerned look in Jasper's eye. Or maybe it was the wine. But before Marly knew what she was doing, she'd reached up and kissed him.

JASPER'S MIND raced as his lips met Marly's. *What the heck?* He knew this was wrong on so many levels, but it felt right. In fact, it felt so right that his head was spinning.

Then he felt it. A slight tingle in his nose, growing stronger and stronger. Abruptly, he pulled himself away from Marly mid-kiss, throwing his head back and letting out a huge sneeze, with another two right behind it. His eyes started to water, and his throat felt scratchy. The citrus perfume. He was having an allergic reaction to Marly's perfume.

Marly sat completely still, looking totally horrified at what had just happened.

"I'm… I'm sorry, Jasper. I think I had a bit too much to drink. I should probably get going." Marly's apology was awkward as she fumbled around to stand up. She looked embarrassed beyond words.

"You don't have to say you're sorry." Jasper held his hand out to her to help her up. Was she apologizing for dropping the plates, falling on the patio, or for kissing him? He hoped it wasn't the latter. He had enjoyed the kiss. He wondered if he should tell her that citrus smells always make him sneeze, but before he could say anything, she spoke up.

"This is a mess." Marly looked down at the puddle of sauce, food, and broken dishes.

Jasper opened his mouth and closed it without saying anything. Did she mean kissing him was a mess? Or the Alfredo sauce strewn all over his terrace? He could tell she was uncomfortable. He wanted to ask her not to leave but wasn't sure she would stay. She looked as if she really wanted to leave.

Maybe she'd just had too much wine and regretted the kiss. Maybe she had a concussion and didn't know what she was doing. Maybe it was best to call it a night and forget all about it. He was mulling this over when a low grumbling sound floated across the terrace. Thunder.

They both looked off in the distance to see a bolt of white lightning light up the sky. The air had become thick with humidity.

"Well, I should go now before it starts to rain." Marly said, dabbing at an Alfredo stain on her shirt and then reaching to pick up one of the plates.

"I can clean this up," Jasper replied, still not wanting her to leave but also not wanting her to get caught in the rain.

Marly grabbed the laptop and mumbled, "Have a good night," before bolting away. As she crossed into his house and out the door, Jasper got the distinct impression she was trying not to break into a full-out run.

MARLY SPILLED out of the elevator, into the lobby. Outside, it was starting to drizzle, and she was glad the laptop was protected, because she wasn't going to hail a cab and head home... she was walking straight to the hospital.

She'd kissed Jasper! What had she been thinking? Too bad the kiss had been amazing, and if what she'd sensed was right, Jasper had felt the same way.

Marly loved her mother. She could *not* fall for Jasper... the very man whom she may have to betray in order to give her mother a chance at life.

Or could she? Earlier, she'd had an idea on how she might be able to satisfy Tanner with new designs and get the money for her mother's operation without betraying Jasper. She was almost sure she could pull it off, but she needed to see those original designs first.

But even if she could pull it off, was Jasper really interested in her? She didn't have a good track record with men, and it still hurt to think of how Derek had betrayed her. Jasper would probably do the same thing. But even so, she still liked the job.

She glanced down at the laptop in her hand. The laptop would give her access, and then all she needed was time. But first, a quick visit to see her mom. She picked up the pace. Too bad she would have to walk past Draconia to get to the hospital, but it couldn't be helped.

Marly turned her blazer collar up around her ears and kept her head down as she headed out of the lobby.

15

Veronica pursed her lips as she hurried down the sidewalk after work. She loved New York, and the fact she could walk to work was wonderful, except on days like today when it was raining.

Everyone and their brother used cabs on days like this, so she knew better than to wait for one. Between the wait and added traffic, it was faster for her to walk, although she wasn't thrilled that her new Valentino shoes were getting wet.

It was humid out, too, and even with her umbrella shielding her hair from the rain, she knew it would start to frizz. She hated that. There was nothing worse than bad hair.

She slowed down as she approached Jasper's building, a move she did every time she passed. More than once, she had just "happened" to bump into him as she was walking by. She looked into the lobby for him and stopped dead in her tracks.

"Watch it!" a woman walking behind her yelled as she bumped into her umbrella.

Veronica started to walk again slowly, timing her pace perfectly so that she would be at the front door of the building when the person stepped outside.

"Marly? Wow. What a surprise! Bumping into you here!" Veronica smiled sarcastically. "Let me guess, there was an urgent suppertime meeting at Jasper's apartment I didn't know about?"

Veronica felt almost giddy at the look on Marly's face. She'd been caught red-handed! Then her giddiness evaporated. This meant that Marly and Jasper really *were* having a fling. Could it be a coincidence that Marly was here?

Her eyes fell on the laptop in Marly's hand. It was the new one she'd had IT set up yesterday. She'd assumed it had been for Jasper, as it was an expensive model with all the latest software and applications... had it been for Marly?

If so, that might explain why she was here. She'd had to pick it up. Veronica felt her confidence flounder as she tried to remember Jasper's instructions on where to send the computer.

The truth was she'd hardly been able to focus on his instructions—her brain had been on a sugar high after gorging on a package of M&M's. She hoped she hadn't screwed up by delivering it to Jasper's home, but if she had, it was all Marly's fault—she was the reason Veronica ate the M&M's in the first place!

Her heart skipped as she saw the look on Marly's face

turn from guilty to pissed off. Marly took a step closer, causing Veronica to back up. The woman looked deranged, especially with the way her hair was sticking up and the rain dripping down her face.

"Who the hell do you think you are, Veronica?" Marly got right up in her face, poking at her with her index finger. "You've treated me like shit since the day I started working at Draconia, and I have been nothing but nice to you. News flash: not everything Jasper does is based off of the calendar you manage for him. And also, you hanging around outside his place after work is hmm ... what's the word I am looking for... pathetic and border-line stalker-like. So take your scrawny ass and frizzy hair out of my face. Have a great night!" And with that, Marly turned and walked away.

Veronica stood, speechless, listening to the rain splatter from her umbrella onto the pavement. Who the hell did Marly West think she was? She would show her, that was for sure.

It was time to fast-track her plan to figure out what Marly had been doing with Tanner Durcotte and expose her to the whole company. She had gone too far now.

MARLY STORMED TOWARD THE HOSPITAL, oblivious to the rain dripping down her collar and soaking her neck. She couldn't believe she'd yelled at Veronica like that. But the girl had it coming. Still, she knew Veronica could make life miserable for her at Draconia, but heck, she was already doing that.

Marly was extra pissed that Veronica's snide remarks had zapped out the last remaining bit of happiness she'd had from her kiss with Jasper. The weight of her mother's illness and what might happen if she was caught passing designs to Tanner already dampened her happiness, and now Veronica came along to steal the rest of it.

Who was Veronica St. James to question her, anyway? She'd dealt with Veronica's type for years, always bullied by them and allowing it. She was almost thirty. It was time she stood up for herself. Which was why she'd lost it and yelled at her.

Marly's lips curled in a smile as she remembered the startled look on Veronica's face. She hadn't been expecting Marly to fight back. Bullies like her never did. Plus, Marly knew that when she called Veronica's hair frizzy it probably ruined her week, as it was always perfect, and today the rain had really done a number on it. *Ha!*

A Darth Vader ringtone blasted from her purse, and Marly's smile snapped into a frown.

Tanner.

What the hell did *he* want? She fished the phone out and looked at the display, her heart crashing against her chest when she read it.

I know the designs you gave me are old. Give me the REAL designs By TOMORROW at 3 PM or the deal is off.

16

Marly threw her phone into her purse, pivoted on her heel, and rushed back toward the Draconia building. The rain pelted down, forming her unruly hair into tight curls. The text she had just read from Tanner demanding she get him the designs the next day capped off her sour mood. She wouldn't even have time to visit her mother at the hospital.

What if her mother took a turn for the worse and she wasn't there?

She stormed through the lobby of Draconia. Since it was after hours, the lobby was practically empty, but she kept her head down anyway. She didn't want to talk to anyone. She hurried to the ladies' room to try and freshen up.

Her hair was in long, tight ringlets that were plastered to her head, thanks to the rain. She secured it in a loose bun and wiped the eyeliner that had smudged under her eyes. What was the point? Most everyone had gone home. No one was here to see what she looked like.

As she slid into the safe haven of her cube, anxiety overwhelmed her. She wasn't a bad person, but what she was about to do was unforgivable. Certainly Jasper would never forgive her. Then again, they'd only shared one nice kiss—so what?

Something tugged at her. It wasn't just the kiss. She'd felt a connection with him that she'd never felt before. They were from such different worlds, but when they'd been going over the designs, it didn't feel that way. They'd been in sync. But what did it matter? Her mother was more important.

Chocolate. She needed chocolate to soothe her nerves. She grabbed some dollar bills from her purse and then headed to the vending machine in the little alcove outside the café.

The vending machine had a lot of choices. Most of it was junk food—chips and candy. She noticed two empty rows where the M&M's usually were. Someone must really have an M&M issue. She hesitated for a minute. The fat girl inside her was pushing her to buy as much junk as she could. She stopped, reminding herself that she had come a long way with her weight loss, and she needed to lay off the crappy food unless she wanted to gain the fifty pounds back.

At the bottom of the machine sat a sparkly row of peppermint patties. She opted for one of those. The minty smell would be refreshing, and they were low in calories compared to everything else. The machine gobbled up her dollar bill, and nothing happened.

Marly glanced at the price again to make sure it wasn't more than one dollar. It wasn't. She hit the button several times, then the change return. Nothing. Her blood started to boil. She inserted another dollar bill. Still nothing, aside from the whirring of the machine as if it were laughing at her.

"Come on!" she yelled at the machine, pushing the top in hopes it would jar the peppermint patty loose somehow. It didn't.

"Stupid piece of shit!" she yelled as tears started to well up in her eyes. She pushed the machine harder, causing it to rock back with a thud. Still the peppermint patty remained in its slot. She pushed again and again, her sobs starting to grow louder as the machine rocked precariously against the wall.

Suddenly, she felt a hand on her shoulder.

"Marly?! Are you okay?" Sarah's voice came from behind her as Marly started to crumble into a ball.

"I can't. I just can't anymore." Marly sputtered the words out in between sobs. She knew she shouldn't be doing this, and definitely not in a public area at work. Thank God no one was around.

Sarah helped Marly stand up.

"Here, let's go sit and talk over there," Sarah said calmly, pointing to a small empty area that had a couch and chairs.

They walked over to it, Marly sniffling as she did so

and wiping her eyes. She must look like hell. How did she keep getting herself into these ridiculous situations?

She sat down in one of the chairs, and Sarah sat across from her on the couch with a horrified look on her face. Marly started to laugh. Slowly then almost hysterically. Sarah soon followed, laughing so hard she couldn't catch her breath.

"Are you that upset that you couldn't get your food that you cried?!" Sarah said in between laughing. This only made Marly laugh harder.

"I can't even begin to tell you what's going on, Sarah. And yes, I really wanted that goddamn peppermint patty!" She was laughing still as she said this.

"What's going on? If you need to talk to someone, I'm here for you," Sarah said sincerely. Marly knew she could trust her.

"Thanks. I guess after what just happened, I need to talk to someone. I just… well… I don't want to put you in an awkward position."

Sarah cocked her head. "How would you put me in an awkward position?"

Marly glanced behind her to make sure no one was there and leaned forward. She was ready to finally tell someone everything she'd been dealing with. Her mother's cancer, Tanner, the designs, even how she'd just kissed Jasper. What the hell. She had nothing more to lose.

17

S arah sat back on the couch, sympathy brimming in her eyes at what Marly had just told her. "Wow. I don't even know what to say. I'm so sorry about your mom."

Marly cringed. She felt better now that she'd unburdened herself, but now she was nervous she'd said too much. "I shouldn't have told you about kissing Jasper. I mean, it's not something I'm proud of. And to top things off, as I was leaving Jasper's tonight, Veronica was right outside his building, and we exchanged some nasty words. So I am sure she will have it in for me now more than ever."

Sarah laughed. "It's okay that you told me. Really. Any idiot could see that you and Jasper have chemistry."

"It was just one kiss. Nothing more is going to happen. Besides, he probably has a string of beautiful women waiting for him," Marly said.

"Nope. He hardly ever dates," Sarah said. "I could

totally see you two together, but that means we have to fix this design issue with Durcotte. I can't believe what a jerk he is. And don't worry about Veronica. She's all bark and no bite."

Marly looked down at the floor. She wasn't the conniving thief that Tanner had asked her to be. But stealing the fall designs from Draconia for Tanner's company was the only chance she had at getting the money to save her mother's life. She had no other choice. He had her backed into a corner.

"Sarah, I hope you know I would never steal designs unless it was a life-or-death situation. I just can't watch my mom die without doing everything I can to save her. I have no idea how I'm going to do it, and I know once I do, I'll have to quit working here."

Marly was close to tears again. The impending doom of failing to provide Tanner with the rest of the drawings weighed heavily on her mind. She was going to have to find the real designs in the database somehow. She would never be able to learn how to use the design editing software to make fake designs as she had planned by Tanner's deadline.

"I know you wouldn't. I'm really sorry about your mom. I can't even begin to imagine what that's like." Sarah's eyes started to mist up. "My parents live in Seattle. I don't see them often, but I talk to my mom almost every day. I can't imagine not being able to do that... especially with my brother being in the mess he's in."

Sarah's brother was in a mess? Marly had been so focused on her own problems that she hadn't noticed her new friend had problems of her own. "What's going on with your brother?"

Sarah waved her hand in the air. "Never mind about that. It's not important. But what *is* important is that I think I know how to get Tanner what he asked for in a way that will probably let you keep your job. Let me help you." She looked at Marly with a mischievous smile.

"No. Sarah, I can't drag you into this. Thank you for wanting to help, but this is *my* mess and I need to get myself out of it. I would never want you to jeopardize your job here."

"Come up to my desk. I want to show you something." Sarah grabbed Marly's arm and led her to the elevator. Marly let Sarah lead her. There was no way she was going to let Sarah get into trouble for her, but she might as well see what she had to say.

"Before I decided to follow my real passion—food—I got my degree in accounting. That was boring, so I took some classes in fashion design before I realized I should really be going to culinary school. I did an internship here for design. That's how I met Jasper. I have all the software still loaded on my computer from when I interned downstairs with the design team," Sarah explained as she clicked on various icons and files on her PC.

"Umm... okay?" Marly raised her brows at Sarah.

Sarah gave her a "don't you get it?" look and lowered her voice to a whisper. "We can take your existing designs and modify them, and you can give *those* to Tanner. They won't be the same designs Draconia is launching. Just tell me what changes you want me to make, and I will do it."

Marly's mind raced. What was Sarah saying?

"Wait. So if I give you my finished designs and mark them up with what I want changed, you can change them with this software? Just like the in-house design team does?"

"Exactly. Tanner would never know. They will have the Draconia seal on each one. There's no way he could know they aren't current designs. And our design team won't know, either, because all they will have are the final ones you've signed off on. You just mark out on each one what you want me to alter, and I can do it, and then you can print them out. No one but us will ever know." She clicked on the print button, and her printer started to spit out the designs Marly had already finished for Draconia.

Hope bloomed in Marly's chest. She could take her designs for the plus line and have Sarah alter them, making them for smaller sizes for Tanner. Of course, the designs for the plus line were geared toward flattering a larger woman's curves, hiding certain flaws, and accentuating what curvy girls had in common. These styles wouldn't look good on a size two. In fact, they would look horrible. But that wouldn't be Marly's issue. She was supposed to deliver designs to Tanner, and that was what she would do. And if people thought he simply did a cheap rip-off of Draconia's new line and it flopped, then so be it.

"I could kiss you!" Marly yelled, hugging Sarah. She

pulled back slowly. "Wait. Sarah, no. I can't let you get involved like this. You could lose your job. This is serious stuff."

"Marly, I already *am* involved in a way. And, really, I want to help you. No one will ever know. Let's just do this, and then you can move on, okay? I mean, technically, you aren't stealing designs. You're changing the ones you already made. Kind of," Sarah said, laughing.

"Okay. But I will repay you. I don't know how or when, Sarah, but I will!" Marly grabbed the folder of designs. It was already late, and she needed to mark them up tonight so they'd be ready for Tanner tomorrow. She gave Sarah another quick hug and bolted for the elevator.

18

M arly looked through the designs for Tanner for the hundredth time, her eyes bloodshot and tired from lack of sleep. She and Sarah had spent hours on these fake designs for Tanner, and she was exhausted. She was riddled with guilt over doing this, but at the same time, she was relieved they were done so she could now focus on finishing her real project at work. She put the designs in a folder and placed them in her laptop bag, focusing her attention on her project.

Feeling famished and realizing that she hadn't eaten any breakfast, Marly decided to head down to the cafeteria to grab some lunch. She walked quickly through the maze of cubes to the elevator, keeping her head down. She knew she looked like the walking dead and just wanted to avoid making eye contact with people for fear of getting stuck in some ridiculously long, unnecessary conversation.

Her heels made a loud clicking noise in the mostly empty cafeteria. The lunch crowd had dwindled, the fake-wood laminate tables with their uncomfortable plastic chairs mostly empty. The smells of grilled beef and onions lingered. Marly's stomach growled. She hurried over to the grill and ordered a steak and cheese.

"Extra mayo, hold the onions?" the grill cook asked her, smiling. Marly suddenly realized she ate the same thing there way too much.

"Yes. Thanks," she replied, smiling back while taking the sub from him. She paid and sat down at a small table by herself and bit into the warm sub, cheese oozing out of it. She knew she should have gotten a salad instead, but nothing beats having a nice gooey steak and cheese when you're stressed out. She took a few more bites and then wrapped the remainder up, the clock on the wall in front of her reminding her she had a meeting with Tanner soon.

Stepping off the elevator, she was headed toward her cube when she noticed a familiar head over the top of the cubes. *Jasper! No!* She almost said it out loud, and made a beeline toward the ladies' room. Rushing inside, she flew across it to the opposite side, as if she were afraid Jasper would come in looking for her. She stood at the sink, her reflection reminding her she still had the sub in her hand. She was standing there looking at it when one of the bathroom stall doors opened and Veronica came walking out.

"Are you eating in here?" Veronica asked her in a

disgusted voice while eyeballing her up and down. "That is so unsanitary, Marly. You really should eat your food someplace else. Unless you don't like people to see that fat-bomb you are eating." She smirked, drying her hands off with a paper towel and then sauntering out of the ladies' room before Marly could think up a witty reply.

Dammit! Of all people to be in here, why the hell did it have to be Veronica?! Marly peeked out the door to make sure the coast was clear of Jasper and scurried to her cube, cursing Veronica under her breath. Didn't Veronica have her own bathroom on her floor?

She sighed as she sat down at her desk, tossing the half-eaten sub to the side. Why was Jasper wandering around this floor anyway? He never ventured far from his office unless it was to go to one of the meeting rooms, the cafeteria, or the gym.

Was he coming to see her?

No, that was a stupid idea. Why would Jasper be lurking around her floor to see her? If he wanted to talk about the project, he'd just call a meeting.

Turning to her computer, she opened her presentation up and spent the next few hours forcing herself to focus on it while her eyes strayed to the clock every five minutes. The time passed agonizingly slowly; she just wanted to get this thing with Tanner over with.

Then, all of a sudden, it was two forty. Time to go. She printed out her final papers for the presentation so that they would be ready to go. Hopefully, the printer wouldn't get stuck and make her late for her meeting with Tanner. How ironic would that be after she clock-watched all day?

She stood up, scanning over the cubes to make sure she didn't see the top of the head of anyone that she wouldn't want to run into, then made a beeline to the printer. From the end of the aisle, she could see pages being spit out one by one. Good, no paper jams.

Things were starting to go her way, and the papers had printed perfectly with no paper jams. She grabbed them and headed back to her cube, skidding to a stop when she saw someone walking down her row.

Jasper? No! Why would he be down here twice in the same afternoon? Wait. Was he at *her* cube?

Marly ducked behind a large potted tree and peeked around the side to see what the hell Jasper was doing. He turned around, and she ducked down so fast she lost her balance and stumbled away from the plant, out into the main aisle.

She scrambled to gain some balance, knocking into the tree, her heart hammering as she caught it just before it tumbled over and alerted the entire floor to her stupidity. Having ninja moves at her size was impossible! She noticed that the supply closet door was ajar and scurried inside, pulling the door closed behind her so Jasper wouldn't walk past and see her inside. The last thing she needed was to be trapped in the supply closet with him.

"Are you following me?" A nasty voice demanded from the dark depths of the room.

Veronica.

Could things get any worse? Marly glanced at the

clock on the wall, her stomach swooping. It was two fifty. If she didn't leave for the meeting with Tanner right now, she would be late.

"No, I am not following you. I needed... Wait, why are you even in here?" Marly asked, realizing there was no reason for Veronica to be in that supply closet. Just like the bathroom, Veronica had her own supply closet near her desk on her own floor.

"It's none of your business, but I ran out of toner." Veronica held up a square container of printer toner as she bumped the door with her bony hip. The door opened a crack.

Veronica turned to scowl at her. "Why are *you* here?"

Marly leaned on the door handle, trying to pull it closed unobtrusively.

Veronica shifted her position, her body now preventing the door from fully shutting. Marly tugged a little harder. Veronica was so skinny, Marly felt sure one good tug on the door would dislodge her from keeping it open.

"I'm... I'm, ah, out of toner. I mean the p-printer was... is..." Marly stuttered through her answer as little beads of sweat started to form on her upper lip.

Pull yourself together!

Veronica looked bewildered. Probably because Marly was acting as if she were hiding from the Mafia and was unable to answer a simple question.

Veronica reached for the handle then noticed Marly's hand was on it. "What are you doing?"

"Me? Nothing. I was just getting toner, like I said."

How long did she need to stall Veronica from opening the door? Jasper would have to walk right past the supply room to get on the elevator. Hopefully, he was already gone.

Veronica rolled her eyes and pushed on the door harder with her butt. It opened further. Marly pulled on the handle.

They both were opening their mouths to say something when the door flew open to reveal Jasper standing on the other side.

JASPER BLINKED into the dark supply room. He thought he'd seen the door moving strangely and wondered if someone had their arms full of supplies and needed help. He hadn't expected to see Marly and Veronica in there together. And why was Marly sweating and Veronica's face red? "Hello, ladies. Is everything okay?"

"Of course, Jasper. I just needed toner for our printer. We're out upstairs," Veronica replied cheerfully then slid her way past him into the hall.

Jasper had been trawling the floor all day trying to catch up with Marly, but now that they were in the supply closet alone, he felt awkward. And embarrassed. Suddenly, he felt like a schoolboy finally getting up the nerve to talk to his crush and then not knowing what to say.

He had butterflies in his stomach, a feeling he wasn't

accustomed to. His mind wandered back to when they had kissed. Marly had seemed to enjoy it. Hell, she was the one that had kissed him first! Now she was staring at her watch and looked like a caged animal wanting to be set free.

"I just needed some toner too," Marly mumbled, trying to shuffle her way out the door.

Really? She didn't have a bottle of toner in her hands. He decided not to ask her about it and instead ask the question he'd been trying to ask her all day.

"Oh. Well, there must be a lot of printing going on around here. Everyone is out of toner," he joked. "Maybe we can go to dinner tonight to talk about it?"

Real smooth. Couldn't he have come up with a better line?

"Tonight? I can't tonight. I have... I'm busy." Marly made her way around him and hurried down the row of cubes, leaving Jasper standing alone in the doorway of the supply closet.

Jasper watched Marly walk away. It actually seemed more like a sprint than a walk. She couldn't wait to get away from him. His stomach plummeted. Apparently, his father had been on to something about not getting too friendly with the employees. And maybe he should have stuck to his previous relationship mantra about putting himself first and just using the relationship for his own needs, because it appeared that Marly West was definitely not interested in him the same way he was interested in her.

VERONICA WAS lucky that she was so skinny, because her small size allowed her to wedge herself in between the gap in the cubicle wall and the wall next to the storage closet so she could eavesdrop on Marly and Jasper's conversation.

And she did *not* like what she'd heard.

Had Jasper just asked frumpy Marly out to dinner?

And had Marly actually said no to him?

She wasn't sure what she had expected to hear, but this certainly wasn't it.

Jasper emerged from the closet, and she shrank back further, terrified he might see her. But he didn't. He walked on toward the elevator, looking down at his shoes as if he were deep in thought. Or depressed. It couldn't be because Marly had turned him down.

Speaking of Marly, she'd been acting awfully strange all day. First she'd eaten her sub in the ladies' room, and just now in the storage room, it had seemed as if she wanted to hide in there. But then when Jasper came, she'd hurried away as if it were on fire.

Did Marly's odd behavior have something to do with her clandestine meetings with Tanner Durcotte?

Veronica removed herself from her hiding place just in time to see Marly rushing out of her cube, her big purse banging against her hips, a large folder under her arm. She was clearly in a hurry, but where was she going? It was only three in the afternoon.

Veronica tossed the toner she had been holding back

into the supply closet and hurried to the stairs just as Marly got in the elevator. Marly was up to something, and Veronica was determined to find out what it was. This could be her chance to get rid of Marly once and for all.

A MILLION THOUGHTS battled for attention in Marly's mind as she rode down in the elevator. Had Jasper just asked her out? Talk about the worst timing ever. She must have sounded like an idiot saying no. Imagine— Jasper Kenney asked her out, and she actually said no. She felt like an idiot. An idiot, a liar, and a cheat who was screwing Jasper over.

Why was this elevator so slow?

She pushed the lobby button over and over, knowing that wouldn't make it get her there any faster.

She was going to be late for her meeting with Tanner, and she just wanted all of this to be over. The anxiety was killing her. She calmed herself by thinking about how her mother would finally be getting the operation. That was all that mattered.

But what if Tanner saw through the designs? What if Jasper found out about it? Since the designs wouldn't hurt Draconia, Jasper might never know. Tanner would never tell that he bought stolen designs, and his company could quite possibly go under. It would actually be a good thing, and Marly hadn't technically screwed Draconia over—she'd helped them.

She and Jasper had a connection. She knew he felt it. But it was stupid to think she could continue to work there and even continue her friendship with Jasper after this. She had to quit, didn't she? Or would Jasper ever understand why she'd had to do it?

19

Tanner Durcotte sat at the restaurant alone, tapping his finger impatiently on the table. Marly was late for their afternoon meeting. He'd texted her with the deadline—three p.m.—and now it was five past three, and she wasn't here. Tanner didn't like tardiness. In fact, he had grown tired of this whole situation. It had taken her far too long to get him these designs. As it was, his staff would have to work twenty-hour days, seven days a week, to get the line out for the Fall Fashion Week show, and that was a huge "if." His company was on the brink of disaster. This line would either save it or put the final nail in the coffin.

He leaned back in his chair with a sigh. He was weary of all of it. Maybe it was best to fold up the fashion company and focus on growing his line of small restaurants. What would Emily have wanted him to do? Images of his late wife threatened to soften his hardened heart, so he pushed them away. Emily was gone. The good times were over.

"Here you go, sir." The waitress placed a small salad in front of him. "Can I get you anything else?"

Tanner shook his head and asked for the bill. He wasn't even hungry, and he didn't care if Marly was, assuming she even showed up. He just wanted the drawings. The waitress placed the bill on the table.

He looked at his watch again and was pulling his phone out to call Marly one more time when he spotted her walking over to the table.

"Well, how nice of you to show up, Marly," he said dryly, leaning back in his chair again and looking at his watch dramatically.

Marly sighed as she sat down. She looked exasperated. Figured. Stupid bitch didn't even appreciate everything he was doing for her.

"Here's what you want, Tanner. All the designs are here. Twenty, to be exact." She slid a folder across the table to him.

Tanner looked over each design, painstakingly. One by one, he reviewed them all. They were exactly what he had hoped for. This was what he needed to keep his company afloat. And by the looks of things, his design team wouldn't need to do a lot to them, either. Change materials or colors, yes, but the measurements must be fine since Draconia catered to the same clientele.

After looking at the last one, he reached into his suit coat, took his checkbook out, and wrote a check to Marly for the agreed-upon amount: one hundred thousand dollars. He slid it across the table to her then stood up and left without saying a word.

―――――――

VERONICA ST. JAMES didn't know what she had just witnessed from her spot behind the elm tree on the sidewalk where she could peek unseen into the café, but she knew it was something. Following Marly had been a genius idea. This meeting with Tanner proved Marly was up to something.

What was in the folder? Was that a check that Durcotte had just handed Marly?

Thanks to smart phones and the great picture-taking capabilities they had, Veronica had captured it all. Jasper would want to know about this. *Try and talk your fat ass out of this one, Marly.*

20

Marly was too busy looking at the check in her hands to care that Tanner had left without saying a word. The smug smile on his face had said it all, anyway. Hopefully, this would be the last time she'd ever see him. Good riddance.

She stared at the check in disbelief. One hundred thousand dollars. So much money. This would save her mom's life!

She couldn't wait to deposit the check then go to the hospital to tell the doctor and her mother, and maybe the whole world, the great news. She felt as though a huge weight had been lifted off of her shoulders.

After depositing the check, Marly practically ran to the hospital, clutching the deposit receipt from the bank as if it were a winning lottery ticket. She dodged the crowds of pedestrian traffic, trying not to knock anyone over as she weaved between them. Her pace never slowed as she entered the hospital and hurried to the cancer wing. She was eager to tell everyone she had done it. She had the money.

Entering her mother's room, she was surprised to see her sitting up in bed, eating red Jell-O.

"Hi, Mom. You're eating?!" Marly ran over and hugged the frail woman. She was all skin and bones. She'd had to have a feeding tube off and on for months due to not being able to eat on her own. Seeing her eating something, even Jell-O, was a big deal.

"Yes. Strawberry. Yum." Her mother managed a little laugh. The constant trickle of morphine made her loopy, and carrying on a real conversation hadn't happened in a long time.

"I have some great news, Mom." Marly reached into her purse for the deposit receipt.

"Well, look at you, eating! This is great that you have some appetite back. Marly, can your news beat this?" Dr. Pratt stood in the doorway, scribbling on a chart while smiling at them both.

"Yes, Dr. Pratt, I actually think it can. I have the money for the procedure. We can do it. My mom can get it done now!" Tears of joy rolled down her face.

Dr. Pratt blinked in surprise. "Marly, this is unbelievable news! I'll work on scheduling a date for the procedure, but you need to go downstairs and work with the financial office to figure out payment. I believe they'll want pre-payment first. Let's not get this held up. I have very high hopes that this is what will make your mother's cancer go into remission. Congratulations. You should be very proud of yourself, Marly."

"Marly?" Her mother's voice was soft, her eyes saying it all. Marly knew she wanted to know how her daughter had been able to get that much money.

"Mom, don't worry. I didn't rob a bank! I have a great job, remember?" Marly laughed, hoping her mother couldn't see through her lie. She would never have allowed Marly to do what she had done to get the money. But she had done it, and her mother would never have to know about it.

Marly squeezed her mother's hand. Everything was going to be okay. Well, at least with her mother's health. She pushed away thoughts of Jasper while she watched her mother slowly drift off to sleep. Even though she was sure the designs wouldn't hurt Draconia, she had lied and deceived him. Could she ever look him in the eye again? Her heart pinched when she remembered the hurt look on his face when she'd rudely brushed him aside to meet with Tanner. She owed him an explanation for that at the very least.

After her mother was asleep, Marly headed to the finance office to handle paying for the procedure. The whole process was surprisingly quick, and Marly was done by four thirty. No sense in going back to work now. Or maybe ever. But she wanted to go back. She wanted to make that presentation and have a chance to explain herself to Jasper.

Once outside, she breathed in the brisk air, deciding that she would talk to Jasper tomorrow and tell him about her mother. Not the Tanner Durcotte part, but the part where the reason Marly had acted strange was because of her mom and the cancer.

Suddenly, her phone went off. It was Sarah.

"Where are you?! Jasper has called a meeting, and everyone's here!" Sarah's voice rose in a frantic pitch. "I've been calling you!"

"Shit. I'm sorry—I was at the hospital. I met with Tanner and got the check. I can be there in ten minutes." Marly broke into a jog. Thank God Draconia was only a few blocks from the hospital.

———

JASPER HAD CALLED the last-minute meeting on purpose. He didn't want Bill and Steve to be able to build a smoke-and-mirrors presentation to cover the truth of the real sales numbers. And now it was getting heated—for several reasons—but the main one being the consistent decline of sales. This was a first in the history of Draconia. He wasn't happy.

"When is the new plus-size line going to be shown to us, Jasper? A lot is riding on that, and I have yet to see anything. Fashion Week is right around the corner. I'd ask the person you put in charge, but she doesn't seem to be here," Bill Henderson asked, making a dig about Marly.

"So everything relies on Marly's line being a success, Bill?" Jasper shot him a cold look. He wanted answers from his managers, not finger pointing. And Bill was right, where the hell was Marly?

"Maybe she's at the sausage cart on the corner," Veronica said rudely, evoking a few laughs. Jasper's glare around the room shut them up. He didn't find it amusing.

"Yes, Jasper, where is she? That girl... Marly, is it? This is important, and she can't fit this into her schedule? Hmmph." Edward Kenney was noticeably irritated. "Since she isn't here and all the answers seem to be with her, then I'm leaving. This was a waste of time." Edward got up and stormed out.

Jasper shook his head. Leave it to Edward to butt in and throw everything off. There was no way the meeting was worth going on with. Everyone seemed to have their own agenda lately, which was finger pointing. He dismissed them all from the room.

Marly burst through the door just as Jasper was getting up to leave.

"Nice of you to show up." His voice was thick with sarcasm.

"I'm sorry. I was...

Jasper stood up.

"I don't want to hear excuses, Marly. I want results. Do you have any idea how big a risk I took, putting you in charge of the plus line? Yet you can't manage to show up for a meeting? People are asking where your designs are. No one has seen them. I need to see the completed designs as soon as possible. And that means tomorrow morning at the weekly meeting. No excuses and no stories about missing materials and all that kind of stupid shit. If you don't have them, then don't bother coming to the meeting."

A steely hand squeezed Jasper's heart at the hurt look on Marly's face. He'd been overly harsh. He was acting just as Edward would act. Just as he *used* to act. Treating people like objects with no thought for their feelings. And part of him knew that he was lashing out at her because of the way she'd brushed him aside earlier. That was no way for a CEO to act.

He sighed and scrubbed his hand through his hair. He was acting like an immature adolescent. This was stupid. They'd only shared *one* kiss… but that night on his patio, it had seemed as if they'd shared a lot more than that. He'd felt something more and thought she had too. Maybe she hadn't. Either way, it was no reason to be a jerk. He should apologize—

"Jasper, there's something I need to…"

The door swung open, and Jasper turned to see one of his oldest and closest friends, Raffe Washburn. His mood lightened.

Raffe's eyes flicked from Jasper to Marly, and a pang of jealousy shot through Jasper. With Raffe's broad shoulders, six-foot height, and male-model good looks, he was like a woman magnet.

"Great to see you!" Raffe clapped Jasper on the back.

"And you, buddy," Jasper knuckle tapped his friend. "Raffe, this is—"

Jasper turned to introduce Raffe to Marly, but she was already sneaking out the other door.

"Marly West," she completed his sentence with a finger wave. "Nice to meet you." She slipped out the door and was gone.

"Was it something I said?" Raffe asked, laughing. "I don't want to interrupt business."

"It was nothing important. I welcome the interruption. It's been too long since we've seen each other." Jasper was glad to see his old friend, but that empty feeling in his gut as he watched Marly walk away told him he'd just screwed up badly.

Hachoo!

"Bless you. Still got those allergies, I see." Raffe handed him a tissue.

Jasper had met Raffe at boarding school. They had both been thirteen, and both from very wealthy families where sending your kids away to school and only seeing them a few days a year was tradition. Though Jasper's mother had wanted him around more, she'd been sick on and off for most of her life, so he spent more time at school than at home.

Jasper and Raffe had bonded almost immediately and had been inseparable until their early twenties, when Raffe had gone to work in London for his family's company, Washburne Industries, one of the largest pharmaceutical companies in the world.

Recently divorced, Raffe had decided to move back to the US to start up a chain of upscale restaurants, something that had been his passion ever since he was a kid. Jasper was interested in partnering with Raffe on this new endeavor for two reasons: first, he knew it would be a success, and second, he wanted to be involved in something other than fashion.

Although he would be a somewhat silent partner with

Raffe, he would be able to learn a few things about the restaurant industry, and that would be a welcome change. He had only ever been involved in the fashion industry on a business level and was getting antsy to try something new.

"Still have time to do dinner?" Raffe asked, walking to the window and looking out.

"Sure. Let me finish up, and we can go. Sarah can keep you company in the meantime." Jasper called to Sarah and handed Raffe off to her.

SARAH TRIED NOT to stare at Raffe as he meandered around her desk while waiting for Jasper. She knew he and Jasper had been friends for a long time, and she'd spoken to him on the phone before but was completely taken aback when she saw him in person. He had to be well over six feet, with the broadest shoulders Sarah had ever seen.

His long black hair was pulled up into one of those man-bun things. Not a look Sarah usually liked, but somehow it seemed to work on him. He wore glasses, but they only seemed to highlight his green eyes. He was also extremely down to earth, which was not at all what Sarah had expected. She could see how he and Jasper were such good friends. They had similar personalities.

"Any suggestions on where to take your boss for dinner tonight?" Raffe asked her.

Really? He was asking her? He owned several five-star restaurants. He had to know all the best places to eat in the city.

"Well, there's a new place that opened up a few blocks away I've heard great things about, very eclectic menu. Five-star review, also. I can book you a table if you want," Sarah suggested, knowing that even though it had a month-long wait list, Raffe and Jasper could get a table in a moment's notice due to who they were.

"Sure. Do you follow this kind of thing? Restaurants?" Raffe asked her, putting the paperweight he had been playing with down.

"Actually, I do. I'm studying to be a chef, so I keep up with all of this kind of thing," Sarah replied, taking a jab at him jokingly.

"Really? A chef, huh?"

"Yes, and she is an excellent cook already," Jasper interrupted Raffe.

"I bet she is," Raffe said.

"Let's go before you get in trouble," Jasper said, winking at Sarah and herding Raffe toward the elevator.

Sarah got back to work as they headed off. Meeting Raffe might be good for her career. He owned restaurants, and maybe that would end up resulting in a job for her. But she still had a lot to learn before she could even consider a chef position. She didn't think about them too long, though. Her mind was on Marly and that meeting. She didn't know what had happened in there, but from the scuttlebutt she heard as people left, it wasn't good.

VERONICA REACHED into her desk drawer and pulled out a handful of M&M's, slowly popping them one by one into her mouth, careful not to smear her perfectly applied red lipstick.

Raffe hadn't even noticed her. He'd been too busy talking to Sarah.

What was the big deal with her?

She was so plain she looked as though she should be selling granola bars on the street corner. Between Marly and Sarah, Veronica wondered if Jasper had any idea how to run this company at all anymore. He was clearly letting riffraff in. But she would be stopping it soon, anyway. Her lips curled into a smile, and she slowly ate another handful of the M&M's.

21

The next morning, Marly awoke more hopeful than she'd been in over a year. The doctor had said he'd call with the time of her mother's operation, and she'd slept with her phone beside the bed. Silly, because of course he wouldn't call at night. He'd said it would likely be later in the afternoon, so she still planned to do her presentation at Draconia. Though she wasn't expecting a call until after the presentation, she'd give her phone to Sarah with permission to answer any calls that came from the hospital just in case.

With the worry about her mother somewhat behind her, she'd done a lot of thinking about her job. She loved the position at Draconia and appreciated Jasper's confidence in her. She was making a name for herself, and she knew her ideas would help the company. She was good at what she did.

So maybe she wouldn't have to quit. No one would recognize the designs she'd given to Tanner as Draconia designs. They would look totally different in the smaller sizes. And, by giving them to Tanner, she was actually helping Draconia since they weren't going to benefit Theorim's bottom line. There was hope for her yet. As for her and Jasper... well... Marly didn't dare think about that.

She picked out her outfit—black slacks and a silk tank top that was loose at the bottom, to hide her stomach. A light, long blazer finished the look. She headed out to work, thankful that her anger took over her pre-meeting anxiety. She was a little miffed about the way Jasper had treated her the day before, but luckily, that only added to her determination to pull off a great presentation of her new designs.

And anyway, what right did she have to be mad at him? She had been sneaking out of work to visit her mother, and she had rudely brushed Jasper off in the hallway when she was on her way to meet Tanner. The realization of what she'd done made her feel ashamed, but the shame was tempered by the joy of seeing her mother sitting up and eating Jell-O. Hopefully after this operation, her mom would be able to do a lot more than that.

Once inside the building, she walked straight to the meeting room instead of going to her cube. People slowly started to trickle in, and she waited for her turn as each manager droned on and on. She hadn't bothered to print handouts. She would walk everyone through each of her designs, showing them on the giant screen in the conference room.

Jasper barely spoke at all during the meeting, and she could sense some tension in the air. She wasn't sure if it was just between the two of them or if it was for the whole group. Things weren't going well at the company, based on what was being presented. The managers were all pointing fingers at each other's departments as to the reason why.

Finally, it was her turn. She went through each design slowly, providing every detail imaginable, including the total overall production cost of the item, recommended store pricing, and estimated profit. After almost two hours, she was done. She had gone through the entire presentation without anyone interrupting, which was very rare in these meetings. She wasn't sure if that was good or bad.

"Well, I have to say what you've done is pretty impressive, Marly. Congratulations," Bill Henderson said. The compliment was totally out of character for him, and he was also actually smiling, which made Marly very suspicious.

"I agree. Marly, the designs are very attractive, not the same ones you tend to see for a plus line. I would wear these," Liz Gershon chimed in from the advertising team. "We can have some fabulous ads based off of these!"

Jasper stood up and cleared his throat. He did not look pleased.

Great. Here it comes. Marly braced herself for negative comments.

But before Jasper could speak, Sarah burst through the door. "Marly! You have to get to the hospital immediately. It's your mom. I already arranged for a driver to take you." Sarah stood in the doorway, holding the door open for Marly with a panicked look on her face.

Marly's heart twisted. Something couldn't go wrong with her mother now—not when she'd just managed to pay for the operation that could save her life! She raced through the door, not caring about her project or that everyone in the room had turned to stare at her. Her only thoughts now were getting to her mother before it was too late.

22

M arly's heart lodged in her throat as she flew through the hospital lobby, rushing toward the cancer wing.

Please let Mom be okay!

She glanced toward the nurses' station as she rushed by. Everyone was going about their business as usual. How could they all be sitting there acting normal when there was an emergency? Why weren't they all in her mother's room?

She slid the last few feet into her mom's room, grabbing onto the door to prevent herself from falling, only to find her mother sleeping peacefully, the only sound in the room the whirring and clicking of the various machines she was hooked up to. Confused, Marly stood there for several minutes catching her breath and then walked back to the nurses' station.

"I had a call that there was an emergency here. What's

going on? My mom is asleep. What's happening? Is she worse?" she asked one of the nurses.

The nurse walked over to a pile of papers, taking out a sealed envelope.

"I'm sorry, Marly. I think there was a mix-up—the call wasn't about your mother. It was was just to let you know you had something to pick up at the desk here." She handed Marly the envelope.

Marly looked at the front. It was from the hospital finance department. She opened the envelope with shaking hands. It was a brief note to contact them immediately regarding payment. The check had bounced. They were not able to approve the procedure.

Marly's heart sank. She read the note again. And then again.

Tanner had screwed her over. That bastard. She stormed back into her mother's room, crushing the paper tightly in her fist along the way. Her mother was still asleep. She looked so peaceful, Marly wasn't going to wake her up and tell her the bad news. She kissed her lightly on the forehead and turned and walked out of the room, tears streaming down her cheeks.

"Marly? Finance called me and told me the funding fell through. I'm so sorry, dear." It was Dr. Pratt's voice.

"I tried." Tears burned her eyes.

"I know you did. You've done everything possible for your mother. I know that. You're a wonderful daughter, Marly. I'm so sorry. There is nothing else we can do." Dr. Pratt's words unleashed a flood of tears.

"I have to go," Marly sputtered, turning away from

him and walking down the hall with her head down. She wanted to die. She wished for the thousandth time that she could trade places with her mother. How could Tanner have done this to her?

Outside the hospital, she realized she had no idea how she would go on. She couldn't get the money to save her mother's life. She'd screwed up everything with Jasper. And if he ever found out what she'd done, even though she'd given Tanner fake designs, she figured she'd be out of a job, too. A job that she loved.

She hated Tanner for screwing her over and realized he could screw her again if he leaked the information that she had given him designs. Worry gnawed at her gut. Would he do that? If he did, she'd be fired, and not only would she be without her mother, but she'd be without a job. She'd lose the townhouse, too.

Despite all that worry, the real thing that tugged at her heart was how she'd screwed up with Jasper. She'd lied, and no relationship could go forward with a lie at its base. What if she told him the truth? Would it set things right?

Her head was filled with too many "what ifs" as she headed toward Draconia. In her heart, she knew she had to come clean with Jasper. Tell him everything. She fumbled around in her purse for her phone and then called Sarah.

"Hey, it's Marly. Can you see if Jasper can meet with me in about half an hour? I decided I am just going to tell him everything."

"What?" Sarah exclaimed. "Are you sure? And how is your mom doing?"

"She's the same. The emergency wasn't about her. It was about the check. It bounced. Tanner screwed me over." Marly could barely say the words out loud. "So I'm just going to tell Jasper everything."

"*What?* That bastard. Oh, Marly, I'm so sorry! But you can't tell Jasper everything. You don't need to. Your designs for Draconia are excellent. Why would you tell Jasper about Tanner? Just tell him about your mom, Marly. That's all he needs to know."

Marly's head was filled with so many things she wasn't thinking straight. Maybe Sarah was right. Why did she have to tell Jasper about Tanner and giving him fake designs? She should just tell him about her mother being sick. But she didn't want his pity. And that was what would happen if she told him. He would get that look on his face that everyone else did when they heard that her mom was dying. And then he would treat her differently and ask, "How is she?" every ten minutes. *Ugh.* But she did owe him an explanation about why she had run out on him. Maybe she should follow Sarah's advice.

"Yeah, maybe you're right," Marly said dejectedly. "I'll see you in a few."

What would she say to Jasper? Sticking to the truth seemed to be the best thing, not just telling him about her mother being sick. Not that that was a lie, either. She knew she could make the plus line a huge success for Draconia if Jasper still wanted her to.

Because she'd rushed out of the meeting, she hadn't

had a chance to hear what he thought about her designs, but the fact the other managers liked them was a huge positive. As far as their personal relationship—well, she assumed that was over as fast as it had started. *If* it had even started. Maybe that was for the best. Why would someone like him ever want to be with someone like her, anyway?

She entered the lobby, still mulling over what exactly to say to Jasper as she made her way upstream against the onslaught of employees going home for the day. She walked right by Veronica without saying a word, noticing that Veronica had popped what seemed to be a handful of candy into her mouth discreetly. Maybe Veronica was the one who had eaten the entire row of M&M's from the vending machine. Marly smiled at the thought of twiggy Veronica hoovering M&M's.

Heading up to Jasper's floor, she texted Sarah so the elevator door could be opened.

Sarah met her at the elevator, hugging her.

"I'm so sorry. I can't believe that shitbag Tanner did that to you," Sarah said angrily.

"Yeah, me, too. I just want to get this over with. Tell Jasper, I mean. I'm just so mentally exhausted." Marly wanted to curl up in a ball, but she knew she had to talk to Jasper now. Maybe if she did, she could at least salvage her job.

"Are you telling him everything? I mean, about Tanner and the drawings?" Sarah asked, looking worried.

"Honestly, I don't even know what I'm going to tell

him. But I promise you your name will never be mentioned."

"I'm not worried about that at all. I understand you need to do what you need to do. He's in his office waiting for you. I have to leave soon to get his kitchen stocked, so text me later and let me know how it goes, okay?" Sarah gave Marly another hug and turned to go to her desk.

Marly headed toward Jasper's office. She paused outside then took a deep breath, walked in, and closed the door behind her. For once, she wasn't concerned with how she looked or if her clothes were too tight and showing off a fat roll. Jasper was at his desk, and he didn't look up.

"Hi," she said softly, taking a seat. "Thanks for meeting with me."

Jasper continued to type on his keyboard and then looked up after several uncomfortable minutes of silence.

"How's your mother? I didn't realize she was in the hospital. Not that you are required to tell me that type of thing," Jasper said quietly.

"Actually, that's what I wanted to talk to you about." How was she going to get this all out without bursting into tears?

Jasper pushed his chair away from his desk, leaned back, and looked at her earnestly. "Okay, go ahead." He stared at her with those piercing blue eyes, and Marly squirmed in her chair. She took a deep breath.

But before she could formulate a sentence, Jasper cut in. "Actually, before you begin, I want to say something. The designs you presented today were excellent. Some of the best I have ever seen. I knew you had it in you from day one, and I am glad I was right. You really pulled it off. The entire company is going to be focusing on your line the next few weeks, and I honestly think it is what will get us out of the red."

A flash of pride heated her cheeks.

She had come a long way from the girl who always kept her head down and tried not to be noticed, and now she'd been instrumental in helping the company. Maybe she *could* save her job.

But Jasper still hadn't mentioned the emergency that ripped her out of the meeting. Was he just politely trying not to be nosey, or did he really not give a crap about anything that happened to her? He probably just didn't give a crap. Maybe the whole idea that they'd had some kind of connection was just an illusion. And if that were the case, maybe she could just accept his compliments and leave. Come back to work tomorrow and focus on her job as if nothing else had happened.

But she'd come here to tell Jasper the truth, and that was what she intended to do.

"Thank you. But there's a few things I need to tell you." She shifted in her seat. Should she tell him about giving Tanner the designs now? Or just tell him about her mother? What was Tanner planning on doing with those designs? Why had he cancelled the check? Maybe he was going to try and blackmail her.

It was probably smarter just to tell Jasper everything, especially if Tanner was going to try to hold it over her head. With everything going on with her mother, she couldn't deal with the stress of lying anymore. Maybe he would understand. And if she got fired, then so be it. She could spend the free time at the hospital with her mom.

Marly gnawed on her bottom lip as Jasper looked at her curiously. Where in the world should she start?

23

J asper's stomach sank as he watched the emotions play over Marly's face. What was she going to tell him? That the kiss had been a mistake? Was it something he'd done? Not done?

This was stupid. He barely knew her. And he'd never felt insecure around women before, not that what they had could even be called a relationship. Not yet, anyway. So why was he feeling so insecure now?

Probably because *this* woman mattered. That was why her brush-off in the hallway had made him act so stupid. She probably had a good reason to run off, maybe something to do with her mom. And if it was, Jasper could hardly blame her—when his mom was still alive, he'd have brushed anyone off if she'd needed him.

Jasper glanced at his mother's photograph. Forget about his budding feelings for Marly—*the company* needed her. He hadn't sneezed once during her presentation of the plus-size line, and if what his mother had always told him was true, that meant his acceptance of the line was the right thing.

She'd always said he sneezed at the perfect thing that was right under his nose *until* he accepted it. He knew his mom's explanation of his oversensitive nose was silly. But his gut instinct after years in the business told him that the designs would help save the company. Marly was talented, and he needed her on board to continue the line even if his personal reasons didn't pan out.

He wished he hadn't acted like such a jerk to her at the meeting. He wasn't being fair to Marly, and he'd better start before he screwed up big time. Something was going on with her mother, and how could he fault her for wanting to keep that private? She'd tell him when she was ready. He wasn't going to pressure her about her mother or the mysterious hospital phone call Sarah had burst into the meeting about.

Right now, though, she looked as if she was really upset and needed some compassion. Jasper's heart melted. Marly probably felt as though she had to explain why she'd brushed him off and why she had been late to the meeting and about the call about her mother. She might even feel that her job was in jeopardy. And *he* had made her feel that way by his actions.

Was he no better than his father, always thinking about the bottom line and not about the *people* that made the company run?

He was going to remedy that right now. No one should have to explain themselves. Whatever was going on with her mother was her business, and he wasn't going to force her to tell him. It was obvious by the look on her face she didn't want to.

She opened her mouth to speak, but he held his palms out to stop her.

"Marly, you don't have to explain anything to me. You've done a great job, and that's what's important." Then, on impulse, he held his hand out to her. "What do you say we have an early dinner to celebrate? I'm starving."

The look of relief on her face told him he'd done the right thing. She gave his hand a hesitant look, and his heart skipped. Would she say no? Did she have other plans? A boyfriend? Then that dazzling smile lit her face, and she slipped her hand into his.

"Thanks. I'm starving too, and I'd love to."

24

M arly's determination to tell Jasper everything wavered over dinner. She wasn't even sure why she'd accepted. She guessed it was because it allowed her to put off telling him the truth. And she liked eating.

It had been a great dinner. Good food. They'd talked nonstop like old friends, but with the excitement of getting to know someone new. A fun time, even though that fun had been dimmed with thoughts of how her mother wouldn't be getting a life-saving operation. Not to mention how she was going to have to confess how she'd snuck around behind his back for the designs.

She'd discovered a lot about him. How his father had been a dominant but somewhat absentee influence on him. How his mother had died when he was in his early twenties. She could tell he still missed her, and it made Marly's eyes burn as she realized that she might not be far from losing her own mother.

He'd also told her about his ex-girlfriends. Flattering

her by telling her how shallow they'd all been, not smart or engaging like her. She didn't know if that was true or just a line, but she liked hearing it, anyway. He hadn't said it in so many words, but she got the impression that most of his exes had been more interested in his money than anything else.

And that was why she'd hesitated in telling him about her mother. She knew he was curious as to the emergency, but he didn't pressure her. He mentioned fleetingly that she could tell him anything, but how could she tell him her mother needed an expensive operation to save her life when all the other women he'd gotten involved with had only been after his money? If she did, he'd just think that Marly was only after his money too. And she wasn't. Over dinner, she'd realized that she wanted much more from him.

After he paid the bill and they were strolling down the sidewalk, she scolded herself for not telling him everything. How could she even expect to have a relationship with him if she didn't tell him about her mom? Or Tanner? But she didn't want to spoil the night. It had been too perfect. Tomorrow, after the managers' meeting. That was it. That was when she would tell him. No more excuses.

Maybe she was just fooling herself that Jasper would understand. That she'd get to keep her job. That there could be something between them. But what the heck, let her be foolish for one more night. Tomorrow, it would all come out.

"Thank you, Jasper. I'm glad we did this. I had a nice time," she said to him as they approached the crosswalk.

"You're welcome. Let's walk this way, and I'll grab my car to take you home." He started toward Draconia.

"No. No, that's okay. I feel like I need a walk right now." Marly wanted the exercise and to clear her head. She was dead tired but had promised herself she would fit exercise in as much as she could.

"What? It's getting late, Marly. Let me drive you," Jasper said.

"No. Really. I had a great time. I just want to walk and get some fresh air. It's been a long day. I will be fine. I walk all the time... and I'll see you tomorrow." She stood on her tiptoes, kissed him lightly on the lips, then turned around to walk home.

25

J asper sat on the patio outside of his office, looking out at the dark sky. The stars were shining brightly. He took a sip of the scotch he had poured himself and thought about Marly.

He couldn't figure her out, no matter how hard he tried. He had always had a problem getting rid of women, and with Marly it was as if he couldn't keep her. She was always running away from him, it seemed.

Dinner had been nice, and the conversation flowed, but he felt as though he had told her all about himself and she really hadn't told him much about her. She'd seemed distant and vague, as if there was something lying under the surface that she didn't want exposed. Then she'd practically run off. Maybe she didn't have the same feelings for him that he had for her. That would be a first.

He walked back inside to his office to look at emails. Nothing but problems. Sales were thirty percent lower this quarter than last quarter. He knew all the fashion houses were having problems, but he didn't know if they were as bad as his. For the first time since he became CEO, he was struggling to run the company.

"Still here?" Edward's voice pulled Jasper out of his thoughts.

"Hey, Dad. Yes, I'm still here. Looking at these less-than-stellar revenue figures."

"I've heard." Edward's voice was laced with disappointment. Jasper hated it when the finance department shared information with Edward. He was entitled to the same information as anyone else on the board of directors, which didn't include the daily sales figures. But since Edward had hired most of the staff, it wasn't realistic for them to not give him what he wanted.

"It's still early in the quarter. The fall lines are coming out, and that should increase sales," Jasper said, trying to sound confident but not really feeling it.

"Well, I hope so, son. I hope you've been focusing on the company and not other things. I'll talk to you tomorrow."

Jasper wondered what Edward meant as he watched him leave. Maybe Edward didn't approve of Jasper being human. Of him having empathy for the employees. To Edward, it was all about the numbers.

Jasper's gut tightened. If he didn't change, he would end up just like Edward. But he *was* changing. Working with Marly had made him see that employees weren't just numbers on a badge. They had ideas and intelligence and lives outside of work that had to be considered.

His nose started to itch. During dinner, he'd tried not to get too close to Marly. He knew her lemony-vanilla scent might start a sneezing fit. When she'd kissed him, it had almost started, but he'd taken a deep breath and said "grapefruit" three times to himself as he'd watched her walk away.

The thing was, watching her walk away like that had given him a sinking feeling. As if she wasn't coming back, despite the great dinner they'd had. His nose started again, an incessant tingle that grew stronger and stronger...

Hachoo!

That was weird. He didn't have the plans in front of him, and Marly was nowhere in sight. There was no citrus in the room. So why was he sneezing?

26

Marly threw herself on her bed and clutched her tear-stained pillow. She hadn't gone home after her meal with Jasper—she'd gone straight to the hospital. Remarkably, her mother was holding her own, but Dr. Pratt had said there wasn't much hope of a full remission without the procedure.

How could one part of her life be so great and the other be so crappy?

Then again, the great part—her job and Jasper—might turn crappy after she confessed what she had done. She hoped Jasper would understand and not hate her. Her small consolation was that she hadn't really betrayed the company. She'd given Tanner those fake designs so that Draconia wouldn't be hurt.

Speaking of which, she wondered why she hadn't heard from Tanner. She'd assumed he had cancelled the check because he'd found out the designs were fakes, but then again, knowing him, he'd probably planned to screw her all along.

But what could she do about that? Complain to the police? Tell them she'd stolen designs for Tanner and he hadn't paid up? She had no recourse. She couldn't believe she'd been stupid enough to fall for it in the first place.

Her phone pinged, and she saw a text from Sarah. She was too tired to answer.

Marly turned over on her side and hugged the pillow. She could catch up with Sarah tomorrow—after she talked to Jasper. With a sigh, she realized that since the managers' meeting was the next day, Jasper would be busy all morning. She'd have to suffer through the whole meeting, rehashing in her head over and over again how she was going to tell him.

Was nothing easy?

27

Marly squirmed in her chair. The weekly managers' meeting was getting uglier by the minute. Edward was even here, which meant things must be really bad. He rarely attended in-house meetings anymore and usually stuck to the board meetings.

Several managers had already been called on the spot, each of them acting nervous and defensive. Jasper hadn't even looked in her direction once, which made Marly feel bad. Then again, his company was falling apart. He had more important things than her to think about.

But even though Jasper had not looked at her, Veronica had been darting smug glares in her direction the whole time. What was that about?

Marly glanced over at the obnoxious assistant. Was she gaining weight? She thought she could see a little fat roll bulging over the top of her Vera Wang skirt. It also looked as if she had a bad case of acne on her face that

she had unsuccessfully tried to cover with makeup.
Marly smiled to herself. Served her right.

Marly tried to focus back on the meeting. It wasn't
easy. Instead of paying attention to what everyone was
saying, she kept mentally reviewing what *she* was going
to say to Jasper later. And the constant looks from
Veronica were distracting.

"No wonder revenue is down. The last ads we ran
were way off base. I have no idea who approved them,
but they were a total waste of money," Bill Henderson
said, taking a swipe at the advertising department.

Veronica put a fresh cup of coffee in front of Jasper
and then placed her fuchsia-nailed fingers on his arm in
a possessive gesture, making sure to give Marly a pointed
glance as she did.

What was she up to?

"I'm pretty sure everyone in this room gave that ad
campaign the thumbs-up, Bill. Including you," Liz
Gershon said, putting Bill in his place. She managed the
ad campaigns. And she was right. Marly clearly remembered everyone in the room approving the ads.

Jasper brushed Veronica's arm off as he shoved up
from his chair, and Marly saw a look of anger pass over
the assistant's face. Veronica sat down, pursing her lips
and fiddling with a folder she had on the table in front of
her. She flipped it open, and Marly craned her neck to
see what was inside. Pictures? What could Veronica
possibly have pictures of that would be relevant to the
meeting? But then she flicked it closed before Marly
could catch more than a glimpse.

"Everyone, quiet down. Let's stop all the internal accusations. This is *our* issue, the people in this room. We need to figure out how to solve it—to lessen it at least, until the new plus line is out in stores. Until then, I've been noticing an increase in the ads that Theorim is running, alluding to some new line for the fall. Anyone have any ideas what that is about?" Jasper already sounded exhausted, and it was only ten a.m.

Marly's gut twisted at the mention of Theorim. Was Tanner actually using the designs? Did he have those commercials in the works before, or had he just ramped up after he'd gotten the designs from Marly? She glanced around the room to see if anyone knew anything about it, but they were all silent, exchanging nervous glances or with their head down, a common sight when meetings got heated.

At the head of the table, Veronica flicked the edge of the folder nervously.

"No one has any idea?" Jasper turned to Liz. "Aren't you supposed to be keeping up on what is going on in the media line?"

"I *have* been. I did see that he had a media blitz going. That's not unusual for this time of year. I mean, we all want to show off our new design lines, right?" Liz said.

Jasper pursed his lips. "Right. But my gut tells me that Theorim is up to something. Hasn't anyone heard any rumors?" He surveyed the room with sharklike intensity. People mumbled and squirmed in their chairs. No one wanted to admit they didn't know what was going on with Theorim.

Suddenly, Veronica bolted up from her chair, pulled a picture out of the folder, and held it in the air. "Why don't you ask Marly what their plans are? She knows the CEO, Tanner Durcotte. Personally, I assume, since she had dinner with him recently."

The room was so quiet that you could have heard a pin drop.

Every head in the room turned to look at Marly, but the only person's face she saw was Jasper's.

He looked as though he had just been kicked in the stomach.

28

J asper sat speechless at the head of the conference room table. What the hell had just happened? He motioned for everyone to leave, including Marly. They eagerly scurried out, each one eyeing the picture that Veronica now held clutched in her hands as if it were a trophy.

Veronica remained in her seat, as did Edward, who had attended the meeting out of concern over the declining sales. Jasper knew Edward must be eating this up.

"Jasper, I'm sorry, but I had to say something. She can't be trusted, for obvious reasons." Veronica was standing up now, in a new short Chanel jacket and skintight Vera Wang pencil skirt. Why did she look so smug?

"Understood," Jasper said sharply.

Veronica had had it in for Marly from the beginning.

Was she making this up to sabotage Marly? But pictures didn't lie.

"And look." Veronica put the picture on the table and pointed. "I didn't get a good picture of it, but it looked like Durcotte handed her a check. Why would he be giving her a check?"

Veronica's words were like ice to Jasper's heart. He needed time to think. He couldn't imagine why Marly would be meeting with Durcotte. Or why he would be giving her a check. Maybe it was all just an innocent lunch. Maybe Marly sold him something on Craigslist. They could be friends or know someone in common... but hadn't Marly told him that she had no idea who Tanner Durcotte was?

"I think she isn't the right fit around here anymore," Veronica continued in a stern tone that implied she was irritated that Jasper hadn't fired Marly on the spot.

"Veronica, stick to making coffee and managing my calendar. I will worry about the business." Jasper stood up and left the room, slamming the door behind him.

VERONICA FLINCHED when the door slammed, and then flicked her eyes over to Edward. He had remained silent the entire time, and Veronica would love to know what he was thinking. Hopefully, something along the lines of how *she* would be much more suitable for his son than that fatty, Marly.

Edward stood up, adjusting the buttons on his suit and running his fingers down his tie.

"I don't want that woman stepping foot in this building again. My son may have a soft spot for her, but I do not. And especially not when the new fall ads hit the newsstand any minute now."

Finally! This was Veronica's opportunity to get rid of Marly West once and for all.

"I couldn't agree with you more, Mr. Kenney. I'd be happy to pack her items up and will have all of her computer access here terminated and key access cut," she replied, trying not to show her enthusiasm.

MARLY GULPED in the steamy city air. She had felt faint when Veronica dropped the bomb about her and Tanner in the meeting. When Jasper had signaled for them to leave, she'd fled the building, too embarrassed to face any of her co-workers, and especially not Jasper.

But now that she'd made it around the block, she realized she couldn't just walk out. She had to go back in and explain herself. Jasper would probably hate her, but she couldn't leave things like this.

She'd made a mess of everything. She couldn't get the money to save her mother's life. She was going to lose the townhouse, and she'd ruined any relationship there was with Jasper. Oh, and she was sure to get fired from her job.

But the part that hurt the worst was losing Jasper's trust. Having him think she'd screwed him over. She had to see him to explain everything. At the very least, he might not be so hurt by her actions if he knew it was all for her mother.

"Excuse me." Veronica's snotty voice clanged through the lobby, stopping Marly as soon as she entered.

Veronica stood in the middle of the vast space flanked by security guards and holding a big cardboard box. A silver-framed photo of Marly's mother stuck out of the top. The box was full of Marly's stuff!

"Your employment here has been terminated, effective immediately," Veronica said in a chipper singsong voice. "Don't let the door hit you in the ass on the way out!"

And with that, she shoved the box into Marly's hands, turned, and walked away, leaving Marly with the two security guards.

Marly stood there in stunned silence for a few heartbeats then turned and walked toward the door. To add to her mortification, the security guards kept pace on either side of her. She kept her eyes down. She could feel people staring at her as the crowd parted, forming a pathway to the doorway.

Exiting the building in front of everyone with her personal effects in a box was humiliating. But what was worse was the fact that Jasper didn't even have the guts to fire her himself. Tears burned her eyes. It was just as well she was getting fired. She must have meant nothing to Jasper, because if she had, wouldn't he have at least given her a chance to explain?

29

J asper paced back and forth in his office. He was angry and confused. What had happened in the meeting made no sense to him at all. He buzzed for Veronica. She was barely in the doorway when he started shooting questions at her.

"How did you happen to see Tanner and Marly together and take pictures without them noticing? Where did this happen? What was her emergency about the other day?" he asked in a rapid-fire manner.

"I, uh, I saw them at Café Lazure on my lunch hour. The emergency was most likely a lie so she could avoid explaining about Tanner, I'm sure."

Jasper stared at Veronica. She looked nervous. What an odd coincidence that she just "happened" to see Marly in the café. Better to find out Marly's side before he jumped to any conclusions.

"Have Marly come up here, now," Jasper said.

"That's… ah… that's kind of difficult to do, as she was fired. Your father told me to take care of it. She left about ten minutes ago."

"*What?* Why would you do that? When is everyone around here going to realize that *I'm* in charge?" Jasper's voice rose so loud that it caused Sarah to peek in his door. Her eyes were large as they flicked from Jasper to Veronica.

"Jasper, please. Marly was meeting with your number-one competitor, and let's face it, it isn't as if she didn't know who he was! Your father is trying to protect the company by firing her," Veronica said.

Sarah stepped into the office, her brows drawn together. "Wait. Marly was fired?"

Veronica turned to her. "Yes, your little friend was fraternizing with the enemy."

"The enemy?" Sarah raised her brows at Jasper.

"Tanner Durcotte, from Theorim." Veronica's quick answers irked Jasper. She should be minding her own business, not throwing Marly under the bus.

"I don't think it's a good idea to jump to conclusions about that, Veronica. And I don't think that *you* need to be the one spreading that around the company," Jasper said.

"Well, I was in the meeting and—"

"Enough," Jasper cut her off. He made a mental note to see if he could transfer her to another department. She clearly had attitude issues. Edward would probably just have fired someone if they showed this kind of disrespect, but Jasper wasn't going to do what Edward would do. Not anymore.

"Jasper, can I speak to you alone, please?" Sarah asked, squeezing her way through the doorway as Veronica tried to block her.

"Sarah, now is not a good time," Jasper said.

"It's about Marly. You need to hear this." Sarah glanced at Veronica, who seemed eager to hear it too.

"Fine. Veronica, you can go back to work," Jasper said. Sarah and Marly had become friends—maybe she knew something that would prove Veronica was wrong about the meeting.

"Jasper, Marly did have a meeting with Tanner Durcotte. Her mother has terminal cancer. The procedure she needs that the doctors feel will cure this isn't approved in the United States yet, so insurance won't cover it. It's a hundred thousand dollars. Tanner told Marly he would give her the money in exchange for the drawings. Draconia's fall line. Marly tormented herself over doing it. She didn't want to betray you. She had to do it for her mother. What she ended up giving him were altered drawings. She couldn't go through with the real thing," Sarah blurted the words out so fast Jasper wasn't sure he heard her correctly.

He sat down in his chair and turned it so he was facing the window. He remained quiet for a long time. "So Marly sold designs to him."

"Yes. No. Well, not really. The designs were fakes. They wouldn't help his company at all. He just *thought* they would. And she had a good reason. You could see why she would do anything to help her mother," Sarah said. "I know you two hit it off. She didn't want to hurt you."

"Why didn't she tell me all this herself?" Jasper asked, his head spinning.

"Really, Jasper? You would have thought she was just after your money. But she was going to tell you. I guess Veronica got to you first."

Jasper's gaze fell on the picture of his mother. Would he have done the same thing if he were in Marly's shoes? Damn right, he would have. But he might not have even been as considerate as Marly. She'd found a way to get the money without hurting Draconia. He might have just sold the designs, he'd have been so desperate to save his mom.

He shot up out of the chair. "Thanks, Sarah. I need to go and make this right."

Jasper knew exactly where Marly would have gone after being fired. To see her mother. Because that was exactly what he would have done.

His mind wandered back to when he was a child, and his own mother being in the hospital with breast cancer. Jasper wanted to be with her all the time, but especially when he was upset. Just sitting in the same room with her was consoling, even though she couldn't talk very much.

He knew how Marly felt, what she was going through. He hurried through the crowds of people to the hospital, eager to see Marly so he could let her know he understood why she'd done what she'd done. For the first time in Jasper's life, he was putting someone else before him.

30

M arly walked slowly down the hospital corridor
to her mother's room. She wasn't going to tell
her anything about what had happened. She just wanted
to sit with her. She had already dropped the box of her
things off at home, where another foreclosure letter from
the bank had been taped to the door.

Every penny she had made went to her mom's care.
Even with insurance, there were deductibles and medicines that weren't covered. It was all over now. She had
no job. Tanner had screwed her on the hundred grand.
She just wanted to sit in silence in her mom's room.

Just as she got to her mother's room, she heard a
familiar voice yell out, "Marly!"

Turning, she saw Jasper hurriedly walking down the
hall toward her. Her gut clenched. He was the *last* person
she wanted to see. After all the work she'd done for
him... her designs would probably save the company,
and he was so spineless that he had *Veronica* fire her. The

only good thing about it was that she didn't have to listen to him now since she no longer worked for him.

"I gave my badge to the security guard," Marly said dryly, turning back around to go to her mother's room.

"Marly, please. I'm not here about the badge. I'm here to talk to you about all of this. Sarah told me everything," Jasper said, following Marly.

Marly stopped. What had Sarah told him, exactly? What did it matter? He had let her get fired. *Fired!* Actually, it was even worse, because Sarah must have told him about her mom, and he would now know how desperately she needed her job, and he'd fired her anyway! He had a lot of balls even coming here!

She turned on him in a fury. "Jasper, go away. You fired me, not even having the guts to do it yourself. I know I should have explained things to you. I was trying to do it the other day and couldn't find the words. But it's just as well. Now I see you only care about yourself. Maybe that was all you ever cared about. Maybe you just wined and dined me for my designs for the plus line. Well, you have them now, so you don't need anything more from me. Good riddance!"

"Marly, let me explain—"

But Marly didn't wait for him to explain. She didn't need an explanation. Jasper was just like everyone else who had screwed her over. Like the kids on the playground when she was little. Like Derek. And Tanner.

She stormed into her mother's room and pulled the door shut. Through the small window beside the door, she could see that one of the nurses stood in the hallway, her arms crossed over her chest, and giving Jasper the side-eye. She must have overheard the argument and was blocking Jasper's way into the room. Good.

Marly pulled the plastic chair around so the back was to the door and sat down beside her mother's bed.

———

JASPER STOOD IN THE CORRIDOR, not knowing what to do. He'd never had a woman reject him before. Was he supposed to go after her? Or respect her words and leave?

"You heard the lady. Get lost." The nurse—one of the few in this wing he'd not yet met—thrust her chin toward the hallway. "Don't make me call security. That young lady has been through enough, and she doesn't need you adding to it."

The nurse was right. Marly didn't want him around, and if he tried to pursue it, it would only add to her troubles.

He turned and slowly walked away, stopping in at the family room he had helped build a few years ago. He slumped down in a chair and put his head in his hands.

"Mr. Jasper! What are you doing here?!" a little voice said. Looking up, Jasper saw Charlie. Charlie was seven years old and had a brain tumor. He was undergoing chemotherapy and had been at the hospital for two months. He was almost always there for Jasper's weekly reading, and a few times, Jasper had even gone to his room and read to him when he was too sick to get up.

"Hi, Charlie. I'm just visiting someone here today." Jasper tried not to let his sadness be visible.

"Oh. You look sad, Mr. Jasper," Charlie said. Kids. They picked up on everything.

"You're a smart boy, Charlie," Jasper said. "I am a little sad about a friend. She's going through a hard time, and I didn't really know about it until now."

"Oh. That's sad. Are you helping her like you helped us?"

"Well, I would like to, Charlie, but she doesn't want my help. She's a bit stubborn."

"Mr. Jasper, sometimes you just help people because you can, and maybe they don't even know about it, but *you* know, and that's all that matters," Charlie said. Words of wisdom from a seven-year-old.

Jasper leaned over and hugged Charlie.

"Charlie, you give great advice, you know that? I have to leave now, but I will see you soon. Okay, buddy?"

"Sure, Mr. Jasper! See you later!" Charlie walked over to the computers, towing his IV beside him.

Jasper walked away, heading downstairs. He knew what he had to do, whether Marly wanted him to or not.

MARLY SAT QUIETLY, watching her mother sleep for hours, the IV full of morphine dripping slowly into her frail body. She didn't know how long her mother had now without the operation. Probably not long. It all seemed so surreal now to her. She wasn't even able to cry. She just had no more tears left.

The nurse came in, smiling when she saw Marly.

"This is so exciting, isn't it?! Such great news for a change. We will start prepping her now for tomorrow." She was unhooking the morphine and filling IV bags with other liquids.

"What are you talking about?" Marly asked, wondering what in the world was going on now. If there was good news, she certainly hadn't heard it.

"The procedure was just approved by finance—it's all set. Your mom can get the treatment she needs now. I thought you knew."

Marly frowned. Maybe the check from Tanner really hadn't bounced, or maybe he'd made good on it after all.

"Are you sure? I mean, I don't know anything about this. I thought the check didn't clear."

"I'm positive. Go speak with Nancy at the nurses' station. She just told me."

Marly stood up slowly, stiff from having sat in the same position for the last few hours. She walked down to the nurses' station and spotted Nancy across the hall, tidying up the family room.

"Nancy, what's going on with my mom? Did the check clear after all? I just want to make sure this is real and not a misunderstanding."

Nancy gave Marly a big grin as she fluffed some of the large pillows on the couches.

"Oh, it's no misunderstanding, Marly. Someone donated the money for your mom's operation anonymously. We can't tell you who paid. Isn't it wonderful?" Nancy winked at Marly. "Your mom sure has a guardian angel."

Marly stood dumbfounded for a few seconds then headed back to her mother's room, hope blooming in her chest. It all seemed too good to be true. Maybe it was a clerical error, or a computer glitch, but if whatever had happened meant her mother got the operation, she wasn't going to question it.

31

R affe Washburn leaned against the mahogany paneling in the elevator at Draconia and looked at the entry form on his phone. The entry was for one of the premier culinary contests in the world. Winning that contest would be a real coup for him and finally prove to his father that he was worth something on his own. His gut clenched. But was he good enough?

Raffe had already made it in the restaurant world by many people's standards. He owned some of the best-rated restaurants on the planet. But that gave him little satisfaction. Anyone with enough money could buy a restaurant and hire talented chefs. What he really wanted was to be recognized as one of the top chefs in the world in his own right. And this contest could help him do that.

Only one problem. The contest was for chef couples, either married or engaged. The thought of getting even close to engaged gave Raffe hives. He wasn't the marrying type. Maybe Jasper could help him figure out a way into the contest, though.

The elevator dinged to a stop, and the doors slid open. He stepped out to the sound of angry female voices.

"I know you got Marly fired on purpose because you want Jasper for yourself!"

Raffe recognized the voice as Sarah, the girl that cooked for Jasper. She seemed nice. Girl-next-door type. Definitely not *his* type, even though she was kind of cute.

"Please. Go back to your desk and do the important things, like making Jasper his meals."

That voice was Jasper's secretary, Veronica. Raffe grimaced as he came around the corner to see her waving her red-lacquered talons in Sarah's face. He didn't know why Jasper kept that girl on—she was a viper if he ever saw one.

"Those meals are some of the best food I've ever eaten!" he cut in, enjoying the angry look that flashed in Veronica's eyes. Apparently, she didn't like anyone sticking up for Sarah. Normally, she would be giving him the once-over, but his comment had pissed her off. Good.

"Jasper's left the building, if you're looking for him," Veronica said dryly.

"Oh, shoot." Raffe glanced over at Jasper's office. Disappointment warred with suspicion in his gut. Jasper had acted a little strange earlier, and it wasn't like him not to be in the office at this time of day. "Any idea where he went? He was acting a little bit off…"

"I don't know where he went. Maybe he's upset because of the way Veronica went behind his back and fired Marly." Sarah folded her arms over her chest and glared at Veronica.

"I did not. Edward told me to." Veronica's beady eyes darted from Sarah to Raffe.

"What happened?" Raffe had noticed his friend had taken an interest in Marly. Jasper had acted casual about it when Raffe had asked, but he knew Jasper well. He had it bad for the brunette... but if she'd gotten fired, that spelled trouble.

Sarah pulled him into Jasper's office despite Veronica's protests. He listened intently, his gut growing heavier as she told him about Marly's sick mother, the fake designs, and how Veronica had outed her in a meeting and then had her fired without Jasper even knowing.

"I haven't been able to contact Marly, and Jasper stormed out. If you could see those two look at each other, you'd know they were meant to be together. And you know Jasper deserves someone good. Now it's all going to be screwed up."

Raffe nibbled his bottom lip. Jasper was one of the best people he knew, and even though Raffe liked having a different girl every week, he knew Jasper really wanted to settle down.

Ding.

They both looked over at Jasper's computer, on which a screen popped up, confirming flight plans for his private jet to leave for London that night.

"It's worse than I thought," Raffe said. "He's actually leaving the country over her."

"What?" Sarah looked from the screen back to him.

"I should have known. Earlier today, he took a humongous wad of cash out of the safe at his penthouse. And now he's flying to Europe. You must be right about him and Marly. He has it bad, and now he's running away. Ever since his mother died, he's run when his feelings got too deep."

"Well, you have to stop him. He needs to be here for Marly and to run the company. Marly's new designs for the fall line are so good that I really think they will pull Draconia out of the sales rut it's been in and get us back on top."

Raffe stared at Sarah. She was right—he couldn't let Jasper screw everything up.

"What do we do?" Raffe pointed at the screen. "Jasper's probably on his way to the airport right now."

JASPER WEAVED through the heavy traffic, pulling his car into the reserved parking space at the Jetway. His phone had been going off nonstop since he'd left the office, and he'd ignored it the entire time. He scrolled through the texts, pausing on one, and then replied, "*Approved.*" The deadline for the fall line—Marly's—was today for the print ads, or they would miss this month's publications entirely. He had been so busy he'd forgotten about the deadline.

"Good evening, Mr. Kenney. Can I take that for you? We should be departing in about twenty minutes."

Jasper nodded and smiled at the baggage handler, who took his bag and brought it onto the private jet he was about to board to head overseas to London. He was glad Draconia had its own jet. Flying commercial right now was not something he would have wanted to do. Too many people, too much noise. He wanted to be left alone with his thoughts, even if they all ended up drifting to Marly.

He slowly climbed up the stairs to enter the jet, stopping to let out a sneeze. Too bad the sneezing was too late. He'd had a good thing right under his nose—Marly —and he'd let her go. He turned off his phone as he settled into the plush leather seat. The only one he wanted to talk to was Marly, and she had made it clear she never wanted to speak to him again.

———

Marly was still in a daze over the anonymous donation when Sarah called her.

"Where are you?" Sarah shrieked into the phone.

"I'm at the hospital. Someone anonymously donated a hundred thousand dollars cash for my mother's procedure! I'm in shock," Marly said, still in disbelief.

Sarah paused on the other end, and Marly was about to ask if she was still there, when she heard, "Oh my God, Marly. I think it was Jasper who paid! Raffe said he took a big wad of cash out of his safe after I told him everything. I hope you don't mind that I told him, but the shit kind of hit the fan here. I don't have time to explain anything now. Jasper's leaving for Europe. Like as in now. You need to get to the airport and talk to him before the plane leaves!"

Marly pulled her phone away from her ear, staring at it in disbelief. What the hell was Sarah talking about? Why would Jasper pay? He had just had her fired!

"Sarah, Jasper had me fired. He didn't pay." But then why had Jasper shown up at the hospital begging her to talk? She felt bad about how she'd treated him, but she couldn't handle much more at the time.

But he'd looked so hurt. Would he really be hurt if he'd fired her? Was the firing a mistake? Could he have been the one that donated the money? He surely had enough.

The nurse had told Marly the money for the operation had come from an "angel"—the same word she'd used to describe Jasper when she'd talked about the family room he had paid for.

Oh my God. Jasper is the donor.

"Sarah, what airport is he flying from?" The doctor had said they would be prepping her mother over the next several hours, and Marly wouldn't be able to see her until just before the operation. She'd have just enough time to get to the airport.

"JFK. The private side. He's taking the Draconia jet. I'll call them and give you clearance so you can get through. Hurry!" Sarah's voice was tight with a mixture of excitement and panic.

Marly flew out the doors of the hospital, her arms flapping frantically to hail a cab. She jumped in and instructed the driver to take her to JFK airport. He grunted and mumbled something about how bad traffic was. She ignored him and called Jasper. He didn't answer. She sent him a text and stared out the window as the cab proceeded at a painfully slow crawl to the airport. Her heart raced.

She had told Jasper to get lost, and he had paid for her mother's operation anyway. He really did care about her. She needed to get to the airport before his plane took off. She needed to fix this.

Veronica called the security desk at the private hangar Draconia leased for the company jet. She had heard the entire conversation between Marly and Sarah, thanks to the intercom system on the phones. She had learned that trick a while ago, and no one ever knew she could listen in.

"Hello, this is Veronica St. James from Jasper Kenney's office at Draconia. I understand that you've been told to grant Marly West access to the plane, but that was incorrect information. She should *not* be allowed beyond the gate if she comes there. Is that understood?" She used her most serious authoritative business tone, but she knew they wouldn't question her. They never did. She had been dealing with them for years.

"Yes, Miss St. James. I understand."

Veronica smirked as she hung up the phone, and reached into her drawer for a handful of M&M's, popping them slowly one by one into her mouth, humming as she did so.

Good luck, Marly. You don't have a chance in hell of stopping Jasper.

AFTER WHAT SEEMED LIKE FOREVER, the cab crept up to the private gate at JFK. Marly threw a wad of money at the cabbie and hit the ground running, heading to the security stand that was in front of the huge gate.

"Hi, I'm Marly West. I need to see Jasper Kenney, from Draconia. I believe that's the jet right there." She pointed to the only jet visible on the private side of the runway, a sleek black-and-silver number. He hadn't left yet. Thank God.

"Sorry, ma'am. You don't have clearance to come in here," the burly security guard said, looking down at some papers on a clipboard.

"That's impossible. The office should have just called. Can you please check again?" Marly craned her neck to see what he was looking at.

"You don't have access, Miss West. I'm positive. Sorry."

Marly whipped her phone out and called Sarah.

Jasper leaned back in the plush leather chair and accepted a glass of wine from the stewardess. He looked out the window, his mind racing with what had happened that day so far. He chuckled at the thought of little Charlie, who had basically been the one who led him to pay for Marly's mother's operation.

He wished Marly had just told him everything up front. Why hadn't she done that?

He was a fool to think they'd had a connection. A fool to feel as if he could open up and tell her things. Things he'd never told other women.

Obviously, Marly didn't feel the same way. Otherwise, she'd have told him about her mother. And needing the money. And Tanner.

He clenched the tiny white-and-blue cocktail napkin in his fist. He never should have let his guard down. That way, he wouldn't have been hurt.

———

"What? Put the guard on the phone," Sarah instructed Marly as she paced back and forth in Jasper's office.

Marly handed the phone to the guard. "My corporate office is on the line for my approval." Never mind it was just Sarah—Marly made it sound as if it was someone in authority as she handed the phone over to the guard.

The guard quirked a brow. "Hello?"

Marly strained forward to hear Sarah's voice.

"Yes, this is Sarah from Jasper Kenney's office. I called you earlier, giving Marly West access. What's the issue?"

"After you called, we took a call from Veronica St. James stating that that was incorrect, and Miss West was not to have access."

It figures! Veronica really would stop at nothing to screw with her.

"That is wrong." Sarah's voice was firm. "Give her access now. She has critical information for Jasper Kenney."

The guard looked at Marly skeptically. "I'm sorry, Sarah. I'm going to have to escalate this. I just can't risk the potential security issue. Please hold."

The guard picked up a phone on the side of the wall of his shack and turned away from Marly. Apparently, "escalating" was something they didn't want everyone to listen in on.

Marly paced back and forth outside the gate, her eyes glued to the shiny black-and-silver jet.

What the hell was going on? She watched the grounds crew milling around and then saw what must have been the pilot and co-pilot enter the plane, and the stairs slowly started to lift up. After a few minutes, the engines started to come to life on the jet. *No!*

"Sorry, Miss West. You're cleared. But I think it's too late now." The security guard handed her her phone back and pushed the button that opened the gate. Marly burst through the gate as soon as it was open enough for her to fit through and ran toward the jet.

She ignored the people yelling at her to stop. The jet hadn't started moving yet. She still had a chance. She must look like a crazy person, but she didn't care.

A COMMOTION outside the jet caught Jasper's eyes. He squinted to see out the window. The plane's wing was blocking his view, but he saw what appeared to be a group of people coming toward the plane... led by... Marly?

Was that really Marly? It couldn't be. He strained to get a better view.

Yes, it was Marly. Running toward the jet. What the hell was going on?

He unbuckled his seat belt and ran to the cockpit, telling them to stop the engines and open the door.

Once the door was opened and the staircase down, he stood at the top. Marly was only a few feet away and then she was bounding up the steps toward him. She flew into his arms, tears streaming down her cheeks.

"I'm so sorry. For everything. And you, you are the anonymous donor for my mom, aren't you?" she sputtered out between sobs.

Jasper's heart crashed as he pulled her in and held her tight, closing his eyes and breathing in the lemon scent of her. His nose twitched just slightly.

He didn't trust himself to talk, so he grabbed her hand and pulled her further in, closing the privacy door between lounge and crew and sitting her down on the couch inside.

"Why didn't you tell me what was going on all this time?" he asked her, wiping the tears from her cheeks.

"What was I supposed to say? I didn't know how to

begin. I guess I just hoped everything would go as planned and you would never find out. I never would have betrayed you. Please believe me. I had to save my mother. I had no other choice."

"I know. Sarah told me everything. I lost my mother to cancer, and I know how desperate it feels. I understand why you did what you had to do."

"But I should have told you." Marly choked out the words.

"It's okay." Jasper leaned over and kissed her. Her lips were warm and soft, and the way she kissed him back made his heart swell. And the best part was, he didn't even sneeze.

He grabbed her hands and pulled her up from the couch. "Come on. We have an important patient in the hospital that needs our support."

32

Tanner Durcotte walked through the doors of Theorim, whistling to himself and nodding hello to the receptionist. He was in a fantastic mood, anticipating the flood of orders that had surely come through overnight from the buyers who had seen his new fall line yesterday when the ads were sent out. He made a quick stop at his office to hang up his coat and then headed down the hallway to the conference room for the customary "day after" meeting, where they reviewed the orders they had received after the first viewing. This was always a good way to estimate sales for fall.

As he entered the large room, it grew quiet. People scattered to their seats, avoiding eye contact.

"Well, I'm quite eager to see the results so far." Tanner's good mood plummeted as he glanced around the table. No one was smiling. Not a good sign.

After a few moments of silence, Belinda Slopes, the head of purchasing, spoke up.

"Well, Mr. Durcotte, errr, things aren't as good as we had hoped." She took a large gulp of water.

"What's the bottom line? How many orders?" Tanner snapped at her.

"None," she replied, her voice quivering.

Tanner stood up, looking around the table.

"This is a joke, right? I am not in the mood, people. Never once, ever, in the history of Theorim have we received nothing for orders after a new line was sent out to print. Can someone tell me what the hell is going on?"

Marcy Nichols, the head of design, spoke up, clearing her throat.

"Instead of purchase orders, we received some feedback. Negative feedback. Overall, the buyers felt the clothing didn't look good on the models, and if it doesn't show well, then no one is going to want to buy it." She looked as if she wanted to add an "I told you so" at the end, which diminished Tanner's mood even further. Even though she had warned him that these designs weren't right, he had insisted they stay as is. They were the designs from Draconia and should be a big hit. Shouldn't they? Either way, he didn't need a snotty attitude from Marcy Nichols.

"Well, that can't be true. That's just one of the buyers' opinions. What about the rest?" Tanner looked around the table.

"I hear pretty much the same from all my sources," Bart Landers said. Everyone else nodded.

Tanner couldn't believe it. What had happened?

Maybe this was a big joke. He glanced at the sales sheet in front of him. No sales. This was no joke.

He stormed out of the conference room, stomped down the hallway to his office, and slammed the door shut. He paced back and forth once inside. With no orders, he was done. They couldn't stay afloat. He had bet everything on this new fall line.

His gaze wandered over to a plaque he had been given by his wife, many years ago when he first started the company. It had one simple word on it. Karma. He had screwed Marly over, and it had come around full circle now to him. He slumped down in his chair and started to sob.

33

M arly melted into the buttery-soft leather couch in Jasper's penthouse, where she was seated with Jasper and Raffe. Raffe had offered to clear out, but Marly insisted he stay. She wanted to thank him for being the one to figure out what was going on and clue Sarah in about the money. If it hadn't been for the two of them, Marly and Jasper might have let the misunderstandings between them fester and never gotten together.

Her mother had made it through surgery the day before with flying colors and was now resting. Jasper had stayed by her side at the hospital the whole time, leaving only for a few hours to tend to business at Draconia. Apparently, the buyers had loved her plus-size line designs, and orders had exceeded expectations.

"I wish I could have seen Veronica's face when you fired her. I never liked her. Too skinny." Raffe leaned forward, his forearms resting on his knees, a tumbler of whiskey cupped in his hands.

Marly felt a stab of pity. Veronica had gotten what she deserved, but Marly still felt a little bit sorry for her. The girl clearly had issues. Maybe her bitchy behavior wasn't really her fault. Then again, Marly could afford to feel generous—she'd gotten the guy, her mother's prognosis was positive, and her job was secure.

"She deserved it!" Sarah yelled from the kitchen, where she was cleaning up from the meal she'd insisted on preparing for them.

"She's right," Jasper said. "Truth is, I was thinking about getting rid of her even before she pulled all this crap."

"I guess you're right. Your father might not have liked that you promoted me after he had me fired, though," Marly said.

Jasper took her hand and squeezed it. "That's too bad. It's about time my father realized that I run the company now." Jasper had opened a new plus-size department and put her in place as VP. "You don't have to worry about him."

Marly gazed into his eyes, deep blue with compassion… and something else she didn't dare think about. Could it really work between them?

"Ahem…" Raffe made a face at them. "It's nice that everything is working out for the two of you. Really. But what about my problem?"

"You mean the culinary contest? That's easy. Just get married," Jasper joked.

Raffe snorted and leaned back in his chair. "You know that's not gonna happen."

During the hours Marly had spent in the hospital with Jasper, he'd told her about Raffe. They'd been best friends since they were boys. Raffe was a playboy, and Jasper had entertained her with stories about some of his funnier exploits.

But looking at Raffe right now, she sensed there was a lot more going on underneath. And, even though he was acting casual about the whole contest, she sensed that it was important to him. He wanted something more than what his father's money could buy. He wanted to prove that he was worthy, and this contest could help.

"You don't actually *have* to get married," Marly said.

"What do you mean?" Raffe asked. "The contest is for chef couples either married or engaged."

"Right, so you could just be engaged, and if the engagement doesn't work out after the contest..." Marly let her voice trail off. She was a little worried that she was getting good at coming up with deceptive plans, but maybe this plan would work out for the best, just like her plan with the designs.

Raffe took a sip of whiskey and pursed his lips. "Okay, I see what you mean. That could work."

"It could," Jasper said. "But where would we find someone with culinary skills that would be willing to pose as his fiancée?"

A dish smashed to the floor in the kitchen. "Shit! Sorry!" Sarah's voice rang out.

Marly's eyes slid in that direction then back to Jasper

and Raffe. "It might take some persuading, but I think I might know someone who would be just perfect."

EPILOGUE

Tanner Durcotte and Veronica St. James shook hands firmly, sizing each other up as they followed the hostess to a private booth in the back of the restaurant.

"Well, I have to say I was quite intrigued when I got your call, Miss St. James," Tanner said, ordering himself a drink as she did the same.

"I'm sure you were. We do seem to have something in common. I thought perhaps we could have a discussion about it."

"Draconia," Tanner said dryly and slowly, as if the word hurt him to say it.

"Yes," Veronica replied, stirring her drink. "I think it's safe to say we both are not the biggest fans of the company or its most meddling employees."

"That would be an understatement," Tanner huffed.

"I was fired by Jasper because of information I gave

him about you and Marly West," Veronica said, trying to read Tanner's facial expression after she said it.

"Miss St. James, there isn't much to tell about Marly West and me. Whatever information you gave Jasper is irrelevant. As I'm sure you've heard, I just had to file for bankruptcy, and Theorim Fashions is nonexistent now."

"I heard. I assume you've also heard that Jasper is branching out, into different businesses. He's partnering with that philandering friend of his, Raffe Washburne, on some restaurant deal." She sensed his surprise. No one knew Jasper was a partner aside from a few people. Veronica only knew from snooping on Raffe's conversations with Jasper and a snitch she still had back at Draconia.

"I wasn't aware of that, but I'm unsure why I would care," Tanner said.

Veronica knew he cared. She knew he hated Jasper, probably even more so now.

"The designs Marly gave you were fakes. She knew they wouldn't work. She cooked that scheme up with Jasper's little personal chef, Sarah Thomas. In the meantime, the real designs gave Draconia the best quarter yet in terms of orders received. Record setting. Marly and Jasper are quite happy about it, I hear."

Tanner scrunched his face up.

"What do you mean, Marly and Jasper?"

"They're a couple. Didn't you know? Yes, an odd couple. And Sarah—I'm unsure if you know her—she's now teaming up with Washburne to win some prestigious cooking award. If they win, it will make his restaurants more popular. It will put a lot of other restaurants out of business." Veronica looked at Tanner innocently and twirled the tiny straw around in her drink.

Veronica could practically hear the wheels turning in Tanner's head. Sure, she'd laid it on a little thick about Washburn's win putting other restaurants out of business. She had no idea if that would happen. But she'd done her homework, and she knew Tanner also owned a few restaurants. She figured the recent happenings with Draconia would make him overly sensitive to being run out of business by Jasper or any of his friends.

Tanner was trying to look calm, but Veronica saw his fist clench around his glass, his face reddening. "So this Sarah girl, she's in on it?"

Veronica nodded.

"She must have been the brains behind the fake-designs plan. Marly's a meek little girl who could never have pulled off such a scheme."

"That's right. She was. And I happen to know a little secret that could take her and Washburne down. It will hurt his restaurants, and that will hurt Jasper and Marly, too." Veronica went in for the kill.

Tanner frowned at her. She could see he was skeptical but interested. She had him right where she wanted him.

"Where are you getting your information from?" he asked.

"I have my sources. The bottom line is, do you want to join me and put them out of business or not?"

****

WILL Veronica and Tanner ruin things for Raffe and Sarah? Find out in "Can't Stand the Heat" - join our email list to get an email when it releases:

http://www.leighanndobbs.com/leighann-dobbs-romance-email-list/

If you want to receive a text message on your cell phone for new releases, text ROMANCE to 88202 (sorry, this only works for US cell phones!)

Join my Facebook Readers group and get special content and the inside scoop on my books:
https://www.facebook.com/groups/ldobbsreaders

ALSO BY LEIGHANN DOBBS

Magical Romance with a Touch of Mystery

***

Something Magical

Curiously Enchanted

————

Contemporary Romance

***

Reluctant Romance

Cozy Mysteries

Silver Hollow

Paranormal Cozy Mystery Series

***

A Spell of Trouble (Book 1)

Spell Disaster (Book 2)

Nothing to Croak About (Book 3)

Mooseamuck Island Cozy Mystery Series

* * *

A Zen For Murder

A Crabby Killer

A Treacherous Treasure

Mystic Notch

Cat Cozy Mystery Series

* * *

Ghostly Paws

A Spirited Tail

A Mew To A Kill

Paws and Effect

Probable Paws

Blackmoore Sisters

Cozy Mystery Series

* * *

Dead Wrong

Dead & Buried

Dead Tide

Buried Secrets

Deadly Intentions

A Grave Mistake

Spell Found

Lexy Baker Cozy Mystery Series

* * *

Lexy Baker Cozy Mystery Series Boxed Set Vol 1 (Books 1-4)

Or buy the books separately:

Killer Cupcakes

Dying For Danish

Murder, Money and Marzipan

3 Bodies and a Biscotti

Brownies, Bodies & Bad Guys

Bake, Battle & Roll

Wedded Blintz

Scones, Skulls & Scams

Ice Cream Murder

Mummified Meringues

Brutal Brulee (Novella)

No Scone Unturned

***

Sweetrock Sweet and Spicy Cowboy Romance

Some Like It Hot

Too Close For Comfort

Regency Romance

* * *

Scandals and Spies Series:

Kissing The Enemy

The Unexpected Series:

An Unexpected Proposal

Dobbs Fancytales:

Dobbs Fancytales Boxed Set Collection

Western Historical Romance

***

Goldwater Creek Mail Order Brides:

Faith

American Mail Order Brides Series:

Chevonne: Bride of Oklahoma

A NOTE FROM THE AUTHOR

We hope you enjoyed reading this book as much as we enjoyed writing it. This is the first in a new series that combines humor, romance and a twist of suspense.

This book has been through many edits with several people and even some software programs, but since nothing is infallible (even the software programs) you might catch a spelling error or mistake and, if you do, we sure would appreciate it if you'd let us know - you can contact Lee at lee@leighanndobbs.com.

Oh, and we love to connect with my readers so please do visit Leighann's private reader group where we can chat and you can find out how to get book discounts and a chance at reading an advanced copy for free.

https://www.facebook.com/groups/ldobbsreaders

Sign up for the VIP reader list and never miss a book release:

http://www.leighanndobbs.com/leighann-dobbs-romance-email-list/

ABOUT THE AUTHORS

USA Today best selling Author, Leighann Dobbs, has had a passion for reading since she was old enough to hold a book but she didn't put pen to paper until much later in life. After a twenty-year career as a software engineer with a few side trips into selling antiques and making jewelry, she realized you can't make a living reading books, so she tried her hand at writing them and discovered she had a passion for that, too! She lives in New Hampshire with her husband, Bruce, their trusty Chihuahua mix, Mojo, and beautiful rescue cat, Kitty.

Together with her sister, Lisa Fenwick, she writes romantic comedy with a twist of suspense. Lisa also lives in New Hampshire with her boyfriend Matt, daughter Alex, two dogs and Sammy the hamster.

Find out about their latest books and how to get discounts on them by signing up at:

http://www.leighanndobbs.com/leighann-dobbs-romance-email-list/

Connect with Leighann on Facebook
http://facebook.com/leighanndobbsbooks

This is a work of fiction.

None of it is real. All names, places, and events are products of the
author's imagination. Any resemblance to real names, places, or events
are purely coincidental, and should not be construed as being real.

IN OVER HER HEAD

Copyright © 2017

Leighann Dobbs Publishing

http://www.leighanndobbs.com

All Rights Reserved.

❀ Created with Vellum

Made in the USA
Columbia, SC
26 May 2018